The Misadventures of Cara and Liam:

The Pyramids of Dahshur

Printed in the United States of America
First Printing 2025

ISBN 978-1-7357335-3-1

Edited by: Jane Spencer
www.janespencereditorial.co.uk

References:
Encyclopedia. Mastaba

https://www.worldhistory.org/article/877/egyptian-afterlife---the-field-of-reeds

https://funkidsjokes.com/mummy-jokes

The Misadventures of Cara and Liam:

The Pyramids of Dahshur

by Dee Ouellette

Contents

Prologue

Have you ever had a younger sibling who knew precisely how to push your buttons? Someone who made you wish you were an only child? Well, I can relate.

My little brother Liam is seven years younger than I am and was born an explorer. Whether he dreams of space travel or getting into mischief in the backyard, adventure is his middle name. And guess who always has to save him? That's right, me—big sister Cara.

Like the time when he was three and decided that a neighbor's wagon full of rainwater was his swimming pool. I found him completely naked, surrounded by laughing kids from the neighborhood, and had to drag him home, screaming. Talk about embarrassing!

Or the time he tied a towel around his neck and attempted to jump off the roof to prove he could fly like Superman. I was both furious and terrified when

I saw him up there. After talking him down, I couldn't decide whether to yell at him or hug him.

When I asked him why he did such dangerous things, he said, "I was trying to get there."

"Where? Where are you trying to get to?" I asked.

"Never mind, you won't understand," he replied. This was the only explanation he gave us until that final outburst on our trip to Egypt. That's when what he was searching for finally came to light.

Yet, despite all his crazy antics, I've realized that sometimes I enjoy the adventures too. This book recounts some of the wild misadventures we experienced during our family trip to the Egyptian tombs in Dahshur.

Chapter 1:
The Book is Here

I snatch the package off the porch, hugging it to my chest. Finally, it arrived—my first book. Well, it isn't just mine; I have a co-author named Bill Bates, explorer extraordinaire. My heart races as I dash into the den and tear open the box. Inside are my freshly printed books.

I pulled one out and examined the cover. It is thrilling to see my picture on the cover of a book I wrote. Beside me stands Mr. Bill Bates, the host of *Exploring the Ancients*, a television series on the Discovery Channel, and my little brother, Liam. We are all dressed in explorer attire: tan shirts and olive-green vests, brown pants, topped off with those ridiculous Indiana Jones hats. Liam completed his outfit with a whip, which he slung through his belt loop in front. The outfits were the photographer's idea, not mine. Ugh, I look like an idiot.

I read the title aloud: "The Misadventures of Cara and Liam: The Pyramid of Dahshur, by Cara O'Connor and Bill Bates. Not bad for a seventeen-year-old girl from Gloucester, Virginia."

"Wow! Nana, Dad, Liam, it's here!" I shouted, and they all came running.

They ooh and aah as they flip through the books, congratulating me again on my great success. I'm in my final year of high school and have become the published author I've always wanted to be. Now, I can check that off my bucket list. But I know my life's adventure is just beginning. I will graduate from high school this year and am enrolled at Boston University to study journalism.

I already have a dream job lined up with Mr. Bates. When I'm not at university, I'll accompany him and document everything in my journals, which we'll use to create stories and books. Best of all, I'll be spending time with his son Ben, whom I adore and who is also enrolled at Boston University.

I say a silent prayer: Jesus, thank you for allowing me this wonderful opportunity.

"Nana, thank you for giving me that journal after Mom died," I say as I hug her. "I never knew I could write until I got that book."

"I knew, honey. I saw the talent God gave you for storytelling and using your imagination, and He told me to give you a journal. So, I did."

The doorbell rings. "I'll get it!" shouts Liam, and off he races to the front door.

Mr. Bates and Ben stand on the porch, saying, "Hello, O'Connor family! Can we come in?"

Liam jumps up and hugs Bill. "Mr. Bates! It's great to see you again. Come in. Hi, Ben."

"Don't I get a hug?" asks Ben. Liam runs over and squeezes him tight. "Okay, bud, you're cutting off my circulation. Man, you've gotten strong."

I went over and embraced Bill. "Hey, partner, did you get your copies of our book?"

"Yes, I did. Are you ready to go? Our plane leaves in three hours."

Ignoring him, I wrap my arms around Ben's neck. Ben smiles and hugs me tightly. I hear someone in the background clearing their throat, a hint from my dad, so I break away from our embrace and answer Mr. Bates. "Yep, all ready to go."

Ben and his dad became like family to us when we vacationed in Egypt two years ago. This led to Mr. Bates and me co-authoring this book, and we've stayed connected ever since. Sometimes, they visit us during their vacation time, especially in the summer during the East Coast surfing competition, where Ben shows off his surfing skills. We also see them at their filming locations, where I began recording their adventures and discoveries in my journals.

"Why can't I go?" asks Liam.

"You know why,' I reply. *The Today Show* only invited us. They want to interview us because of the book. You didn't write it; we did."

"I may not have written the book, but I certainly lived it!"

"We all lived it, but the TV people don't want to pay for all of us to come. How about I try to convince Dad to book a trip to a theme park for our next vacay?"

"Heck yeah!" Liam replies, and we all laugh.

"Well, actually," says Bill, "the show people called me early this morning and asked if we could bring Liam too. After all, his name is on the book title, and he was responsible for the discoveries, too. For once, his misadventures turned out not to be a mishap."

Liam's eyes are wide with excitement. "Really? Can I go, Dad?"

In my head, I'm screaming. No, no, no! I don't want to have to babysit Liam; it always ends in disaster. I shut my eyes tight, hold out my hand, and tried to use the power of the Force—say no, Dad, this is not the boy they are looking for; move along.

"They sent a plane ticket for Liam, in case you said yes," says Ben.

Crap!

"If they have a plane ticket for you, I think you should go. Nana, can you help him pack?" Dad asks.

"Sure. Come on, Liam, and this time, make sure

you pack more than just one pair of underwear."

"Nana, you're embarrassing me."

Nana just chuckles as they march up the stairs to his bedroom.

I shake my head. "You have got to be kidding me! Really, Dad, you coulda said no."

Dad gives me an evil grin and a laugh. "Now you have an annoying chaperone."

I cross my arms and snort in frustration. Why, oh why, can't I ever get a break from this kid?

We sit down to wait, but it isn't long before Nana has Liam packed and ready to go. They come down the stairs about ten minutes later, with Liam jumping excitedly and wearing his Bill Bates mini-me outfit. He goes over and stands next to Bill. They look like twins.

Bill grins. "I remember posing for the cover in matching outfits, Cara; get yours, and we'll wear them on camera!"

"Not for all the money in the world."

"Are you sure? I thought we looked great." Outside, a horn sounds. "Okay, it sounds like Uber is ready to go. We gotta hustle," says Bill as he grabs my bags next to the front door.

"Now, do you have everything I taught you to bring on a plane flight?" asks Nana.

I roll my eyes. "Yes, Nana."

"You'll have to share those things with your brother since I don't have time to get them to him."

I sigh. "Fine, come on, Liam, let's go."

"Do you have enough cash for shopping?" asks Dad.

"Well, now that you mention it, you could put a few hundred dollars more on my debit card," I suggest. "After all, New York is really expensive, and I now have Liam with me."

Now, my dad rolls his eyes. "Get outta here, kid, before I change my mind. And spend some of that money on your kid brother. One more thing—no sneaking out to nightclubs when Bill falls asleep."

"Oh brother, I guess we'll never live that down," Ben says.

Dad crossed his arms and gave Ben that look. "I'm serious, young man!"

Bill crosses his arms and stands beside Dad, saying, "Yeah, we mean it!"

Ben gulps and stands at attention. "Sirs, yes, sirs." I giggle, smile, and walk past Ben, who shot me a glare.

"That goes for you, too, young lady," Dad says. I don't look back; I simply wave goodbye over my shoulder and hop into the Uber.

Before long, we're off to Newport News Airport for a direct flight to New York City. On the plane, Ben whispers in my ear, "Your dad is scary."

"You've mentioned that before. Remember when we got caught sneaking out to the pub in England, and they decided to enlist you in the navy and make my dad your commanding officer?" Ben gulped again and nodded.

I laugh and snuggle against his arm. "Don't worry, I'll protect you from the big, bad, daddy. He's like putty in my hands."

Ben and I sit quietly together while poor Bill sits with Liam and has to field his endless questions. I chuckled, thinking he should have told *The Today Show* that Liam couldn't come.

As we travel, I reflect on the last two years and wonder how I got here. How did I go from the small town of Gloucester, Virginia, to an adventure in England and Egypt that led to two significant historical discoveries? From there, I collaborated with an amazing and famous Hollywood star on a bestselling book.

It all started when I introduced Liam to the TV series *Exploring the Ancients* with Bill Bates, the day after our trip to the mall to get new shoes…

Chapter 2:
The Great Shoe Shopping Misadventure

Dear Journal,

Yesterday, Nana took us shopping for shoes. We sat Liam in a chair with a new comic book and a snack, but it didn't hold his attention for long. This day will forever be known in our family history as 'The Great Shoe Shopping Misadventure.'

"Girls!" Liam muttered to himself. "What is it about shoes anyway? I could understand if they were cowboy boots, cool hiking boots, or even soccer cleats, but high heels are just silly." Liam was eight, with sandy reddish-blond hair, blue eyes, and freckles all over. He was small for his age and always full of questions, curious about everything under the sun.

He scooted out of the chair and tiptoed to the door that led to the mall. He looked back to see if we noticed, but we didn't. Smiling, he walked down the mall corridor, checking out the stores, watching the people, and seeking adventure.

Liam continued through the mall and noticed a mall cop in a golf cart. The cop stopped to talk to some people and grab a snack at Dairy Queen. He plugged the cart into an electrical outlet to recharge, and Liam watched him walk away, leaving the keys in the cart.

Liam thought it would be fun to drive the cart out of the mall and head to his favorite museum, the Mariners Museum. This museum displayed a wide variety of boats. Perhaps he could borrow one and use that boat to find what he was looking for. Now, that would be a great adventure. He looked around to see if anyone was watching and hopped into the cart.

Not wanting to be accused of stealing the cart, Liam searched for the cop to ask permission to use it. The cop was ordering ice cream at the Dairy Queen counter, his back turned to the cart. Liam leaned out and whispered, "Hey, mister, can I borrow your cart?"

When the man didn't answer, Liam shrugged and said, "He didn't say no. Let's see. How do you drive this thing?"

Instructions were taped to the dashboard next to the keyhole.

Turn the key to the right to move forward and to the left to move backward. Step on the right pedal to accelerate and the left to stop.

Liam turned the key to the right. He tried sitting in the seat to drive but couldn't reach the pedals, so he stood up, grabbed the wheel, and stomped on the right pedal. He had to drive standing up, but it was working. He raced down the mall, trying to avoid people and kiosks. The cart's plug was yanked out of the wall and clattered on the floor as it dragged behind. Shoppers dived out of his way, jumped back into doorways, or yelled at him to stop or watch out.

But he couldn't hear them. In his head, he heard the theme music from Indiana Jones. Then he started singing it out loud, "Ta, di, dump, da, ta, di da, ta, di, dump, da, ta, di, da, da, da!" He hit a trash can and knocked it over, spilling trash everywhere. "Oops, sorry," he called over his shoulder.

As he sang, he looked for the mall exit door. "Ta, di, dump, da, ta, di da, ta, di, dump, da, ta, di, da, da, da!" He swerved toward a group of women with bags of merchandise; they threw their bags up in the air, screamed, and ran to get out of his way. Stuff went everywhere, and one of the cart's wheels ran over a bag, dragging it for a few feet before it was released. "Sorry, my bad," he yelled at the woman. "Ta, di, dump, da, ta, di da, ta, di, dump, da, ta, di, da, da, da!"

He was nearing the end of the mall, so he stopped singing and concentrated on looking for the door that led outside. But he couldn't find it. Still moving at full speed, he whipped the steering wheel around to turn back the other way. The cart leaned and went up on two wheels. Liam gripped the steering wheel tightly and hung on for dear life. "Whoa!" he said.

Then, the cart plopped back down on all four wheels. "Awesome!" he shouted. He continued to sing, "Ta, di, dump, da, ta, di da, ta, di, dump, da, ta, di, da, da, da!"

The mall cop had returned to where he had left his cart, licking his double scoop of ice cream. He realized it was gone, looked around, and saw Liam racing down the corridor on the cart. He yelled, "Hey, come back here, kid!" Then he took off after him, dropping his ice cream as he ran.

Liam was singing at the top of his lungs when he noticed the mall cop. "Ta, di, dump, da, ta, di da, ta, di, dump, da, ta, di, da, da, da! Uh oh! Oh, snap!"

"Stop!" the guard yelled, and he reached out to grab hold of the back of the cart. He almost touched it, when Liam took his foot off the right pedal and stomped on the left. Liam flew into the air but firmly gripped the steering wheel, so he plopped back down inside the cart. The security guard slammed into the back of the halted cart and fell to the mall floor, with the wind knocked out of him.

Liam jumped off the cart and leaned over the guard. "Thanks, mister, that was amazing! I've always wanted to drive one of those things. I've gotta go find my grandma now. Bye!"

He raced off as the guard struggled to get up. People rushed to help him, but he waved them away.

They asked, "Are you okay?" but he was gasping for air and unable to respond.

He held up one finger as if to say "Hold on," and everyone waited until he caught his breath. Finally, he stood and whispered, "Which way did that little punk go?"

Everyone pointed, and the cop was off.

Mom passed away when he was four and I was eleven. I tried to take care of Liam, the house, and myself, but Dad said we needed help. So, Nana moved in. That was four years ago.

Nana is a strong, independent woman. Her hair is a blend of white, gray, red, and brown, and her eyes are a hazel color. We love her, and I am so glad she's here with us.

Liam means "strong-willed warrior," and boy, is he strong-willed. He always does whatever he wants, regardless of the punishment he faces. He constantly wanders off and tries new things that put him in danger.

Our last name means "champion." The O'Connors' ancestors were Irish royalty. But I never felt like a princess. I have long reddish-brown hair, freckles, and green eyes. I don't feel attractive, and I'm a little shy and awkward. Dad says I'm beautiful, but his opinion doesn't count. All dads say that to their daughters.

Nana was paying for our items at the register. She turned toward the chair, where Liam should have been, and said, "Okay, buddy, we're finally ready to go. Liam? Liam? Where did he go now?"

I closed my eyes and sighed deeply. "He's probably off on another great misadventure."

"Well, you better go look for him," Nana replied.

I walked into the mall and looked one way, but there was no sign of Liam. Then I looked the other way. Liam was racing toward me, waving and smiling, with a mall cop behind him yelling, "Stop, kid!"

"Hey, sis," Liam yelled. "You should've seen me driving the golf cart. It was awesome!"

I put my hands on my hips and asked, "Liam, what did you do?"

Liam stuffed his hands in his pockets, looking guilty as he stared at the floor. Using his foot to draw a circle on the ground, he muttered, "Nothin', sis, honest! I just took the golf cart for a short ride around the mall."

"What golf cart? Where did you get it?"

"I asked that guy who owns the cart if I could borrow it. He didn't say nothin', so I figured it was okay. I didn't even get outside."

"Why were you going outside?"

"So, I could get to Mariners Museum, of course."

"Where is this guy?"

Liam pointed at the mall cop, who had slid up beside him and was bent over, heaving and gasping for breath. He was sweating profusely and extremely overweight, probably because he sat in a cart all day. He held up one finger, and we waited for him to recover.

"This kid stole my cart," he finally gasped out.

"Did not! I only borrowed it," Liam yelled.

Nana came out of the store with our packages. "What's going on here?"

While the mall cop heaved and gasped, checking his pulse in fear of having a heart attack, Liam glared at him with his arms crossed.

"Nana, it seems Liam borrowed the mall cop's cart without permission," I replied.

The mall cop panted, "He stole it!"

"Did not!" Liam yelled.

"Seems Liam wanted to take the cart outside and drive it to the Mariners Museum," I added.

Nana leaned over and whispered to me, "Today's life lesson is, when in doubt, always blame the adult."

Nana always taught us life lessons, even when we didn't want them, or they didn't make sense. What did she mean by that?

She turned to the cop and said, "So, you endangered my grandson, this innocent little child, by letting him drive your golf cart down a busy highway to Mariners Museum? Are you crazy? He could have been killed. The traffic on that highway goes sixty miles an hour."

The mall cop looked shocked and stuttered. "Wait, I didn't give him permission—"

Nana interrupted. "I should call your boss and report you. I should call social services; you may have committed child endangerment," she yelled, drawing a crowd.

I covered my mouth to keep from bursting out laughing. Now I got it: When in doubt, blame the adult.

"Where are the cops when you need them? Where's my cell phone? Someone google the social services number."

The mall cop looked around at the glaring crowd. "Wait, no, I didn't," he stuttered.

"Hey, mister," Liam said, pointing down the mall to the man's cart. "That lady is taking your cart."

The mall cop whipped around just in time to see an elderly woman speeding down the mall in his cart, yelling, "Whee!"

"Hey, lady, come back!" the cop shouted as he raced after her.

I grabbed Liam's arm. "Time to go," I said, and the three of us marched out of the mall.

"That was awesome!" Liam exclaimed, looking up at me and Nana, who glared back at him. Sighing, he added, "Yeah, I know, I'm grounded. Sheesh, can't a guy have any fun?"

"Fun! You think this is fun?" I yelled. "It's not fun; it's embarrassing. Why do you engage in these crazy misadventures?"

"Mariners has many boats, and I thought maybe I could borrow one. I have to find it," Liam muttered to himself.

"Find what?"

"Nothing, never mind. I have to do this by myself."

"Do what?" I said, but Liam just walked away without another word. I had no idea what was going on in his head or what he was searching for.

Later that night, I found Liam slumped in a chair, staring at a blank TV. "How long are you grounded for?"

"Nana said I can't go anywhere for the next two weeks."

"Ouch, that's tough."

"Yeah, it is, because Danny's having a birthday party next week, and I can't go. Plus, I'm only allowed to watch boring educational shows. No *Batman*, *Iron Man*, nothing."

I felt sorry for him. "Okay, look, I have an educational show you might actually like. It's called *Exploring the Ancients* with Bill Bates. He's a man who embarks on extraordinary adventures, uncovering ancient treasures, exploring castles, caves, and pyramids, and attempting to solve the world's greatest mysteries.

"Sounds boring."

"It's not; it's on the Discovery Channel, so it's sorta educational. Best of all, he looks and dresses like Indiana Jones. He even wears the same kind of hat as Indy—a fedora." Well, that last remark got Liam to sit up straight and look excited.

"Really? Can we watch it right now?"

"Let me check. Nana!" I yelled.

Nana popped her head in from the kitchen. "You yelled?"

"Can Liam and I watch *Bill Bates: Exploring the Ancients*?"

"I love him! Sure, I wanna watch too. I'll make some popcorn."

We spent the rest of the evening—and every evening for a week—binge-watching that show. Bill Bates became Liam's hero. He even started dressing like him, wearing cargo pants, untucked shirts with front pockets, and a fedora on his head. He even began carrying a whip like Indiana Jones because, as he tells it, Mr. Bates and Indy are both his heroes. When he tried to take the whip to school, however, his teacher considered it a weapon and banned it from school property.

Liam often said, "One day, I'm going on a great adventure with Mr. Bates."

I didn't realize how true that statement would be. Not long after this, we found ourselves immersed in our favorite TV series, embarking on a terrifying real-life misadventure.

Chapter 3:
A Surprise Awaits

"Nana, Liam, come on; Dad's Zoom starts in two minutes," I yelled up the stairs.

"Coming," I heard them respond.

I was excited to see Dad and talk to him. It had been two weeks since he connected with us by Zoom. I was hoping he'd tell us when he was coming home. It had been months and months. Sometimes, I thought he volunteered to go on deployment to get away from us and grieve for my mother alone. We never talked about her. We all pretended that everything was fine.

Nana and Liam plopped down beside me, and we scooted close together to view the screen just as Dad opened the Zoom session.

Liam burst into a smile and waved at the screen. "Dad! Hi, Dad!"

"Hi, son, Cara, Mom, how are you all?"

We all talked at once, declaring we were okay and asking him how he was doing.

"Wait, wait, let's take turns talking so I can hear you all."

"Me first," shouted Liam. "Guess what, Dad? I went online and learned how to use my whip. I've been practicing in the backyard. I got really good at snapping plastic bottles off the picnic table. I'm gonna protect Nana and Cara from any bad guys that come around here. I even snapped the whip around my friend Danny's wrist and yanked him off his feet. He flopped right down on the ground."

"You did what?" I asked.

"Oh, Liam, no," said Nana

"Oh, son, you should never practice on living beings, especially your friends. I don't mind you learning how to use the whip, but you must remember that it is a weapon. Practice on cans, boxes, and stuffed animals, not on people or animals.

"Okay, Dad, sorry. Danny did cry a little. I felt really bad that I hurt his wrist; it was really red. I gave him my Pikachu Pokémon card and told him I was sorry, so we're still friends. I know better than to test my whip on him now. Next, I'm gonna learn how to snap the whip up, grab a branch on the tree, and swing on it like Tarzan. I'll be just like my hero, Indiana Jones!"

I rolled my eyes.

"Liam, that only happens in the movies; it's not real."

"Yes, it is!"

"No, it's not!"

"Come on, kids. Stop bickering. We only have a few minutes to talk to your dad," Nana said.

Dad smiled. "I miss you guys; even your bickering is music to my ears."

"Oh, brother. If you were here and had to listen to his nonsense and constant questions every day, you wouldn't say that," I complained. "Can I talk now?"

"Go ahead," Dad replied.

"I know we have a strict no-dating-before-you're-sixteen policy, but a boy in my school asked me to the senior prom. Can I go? Please."

"So, is this kid a senior? Is he eighteen?"

"Well, yeah, but—"

"Then no."

"But Dad, that's only three years older than me. He's a great guy, not a punk, very polite."

"Nope."

I slumped back in my chair, crossed my arms, and muttered under my breath, "So unfair."

For the next few minutes, Nana and Dad discussed household matters: bills, taxes, where the measuring tape was in the tool shed, etcetera. I tuned out.

"Okay, guys, I have some exciting news to share with you."

We all sat up and gave Dad our undivided attention.

"Are you coming home?" I asked, hoping.

"No, but you're coming to me. I've booked flights for you all to join me in the Middle East. We'll head to Egypt to tour the pyramids in Giza!"

We all responded with cheers.

"Really?" Liam asked.

"That's amazing," Nana remarked.

"Wow, Dad, this is awesome; when are we going?"

"During spring break and the whole week after. Mom, can you get permission from the school for them to hand in their schoolwork early?"

"I'll see what I can do," Nana replied.

"I have another surprise for you, too, but I'm going to make you wait until you get here to tell you what it is."

"What is it, Dad? Are we gonna ride camels? Can we go on an adventure when we get there? Maybe find a mummy or climb the pyramids like a mountain, or—"

Liam would have gone on for hours if Dad hadn't interrupted.

"Wait, Liam, it's a secret; I'll tell you when you arrive."

"Can you give us a hint?" I asked.

"No, but you'll love it."

"It's a puppy!" Liam yelled.

Dad laughed. "Sorry, bud, it's not a puppy. We're out of time, kids. I love you all. I'll talk to you again next week if I can get time on the Internet. Be good for Nana. Bye for now."

"Wait, one more thing, son," said Nana. "There are still some boxes in the garage with Laura's name on them. They're falling apart, and we need to go through them. I don't want any memorial items to be destroyed by the elements. I know it's hard, but I would gladly go through them myself; I'd like Cara to help me, if that's okay with both of you."

The entire joyful atmosphere shifted as soon as my mom's name was mentioned. Sadness filled the room, and the three of us stared at the floor without responding to Nana.

"Okay," she said. "I suppose we can wait. But everyone, one day, we need to discuss this. We don't want to forget her, but we have to keep moving forward with our lives."

"We will, Mom, soon, I promise. I have to go now; others are waiting to go online. Love you, bye. Look for the airline tickets in your email, Cara."

"Got it, Dad. Bye, love you, miss you."

And he was gone. We all sat still for a few minutes, lost in our own thoughts.

Nana sensed the need to change the mood and suggested, "Who's ready to pop some corn and watch *Exploring the Ancients*?"

Liam jumped up and ran to the TV, shouting, "Yes!"

Nana headed into the kitchen, and I sat there for a few more minutes, contemplating what secret Dad could be talking about. Was he dating someone? Were we getting a new mom? Was he transferring to another ship? Could he be coming home? I doubted the navy would let him come home; he was an experienced, decorated ship captain. I got up and joined Liam in front of the TV. As the show began, the title of this episode captured where our family stood: "Remembering the Departed: How the Ancients Buried Their Dead."

Chapter 4:
Meeting Our Hero

When my mother died, Nana gave me a journal and suggested that writing my thoughts in it would help me cope with my grief. She was right; it has helped me a lot. I am now on my tenth journal. I write about everything: my hopes, dreams, problems, prayers, and stories. I discovered that I love writing. I spend a lot of time detailing Liam's misadventures. No matter how hard I try to avoid his crazy antics, he always pulls me in, usually to rescue him. A week before the Zoom call with Dad, I wrote this:

Dear Journal,

Yesterday should have been a celebration. My team won the soccer tournament, but instead, it turned into a rescue mission for Liam, thanks to yet another one of his ridiculous misadventures. I mean, I scored the winning goal, for crying out loud! Yet, instead of enjoying pizza with my team-mates, I had to help the fire department find my missing little brother. I was so embar-rassed!

And where was he? In the cornfield. The corn was so tall that we couldn't see him, and he was so deep in there that he couldn't hear us calling him. The firemen had to call in a drone operator. It took hours to find him, and I missed the whole pizza party. I was so mad at him that I went home, locked myself in my room, and wouldn't talk to him.

I mean, seriously, why would he wander off into a cornfield? He said he was looking for "it." What is "it"? He still won't say what he is searching for but insists that we will all be happy again when he finds it. Jesus, please help me with this kid. Please keep him from going on his crazy misadventures.

But things were about to change for the better. Today, I was writing about how excited I was to see my dad.

Dear Journal,

I can't wait to hug my dad. I miss him so much. Since he's been deployed in the Middle East, we've been able to see and talk to him via Zoom, but it's still not as

comforting as holding his hand or snug-
gling next to him on the couch to watch a
movie. He's arranged to meet us in Egypt
with a layover in London. We'll be gone for
two weeks.

I can't wait to see the pyramids; they're
number one on my bucket list. This must be
why Liam loves adventures. It's so exciting—
my first plane ride, my first trip to a foreign
country. I wonder what else I'll check off my
bucket list before returning.

Then, I closed my journal and stuffed it into my carry-on backpack. I was looking forward to journaling in another country. I had everything packed. I reviewed my luggage and Nana's latest life lessons on traveling. First, keep essentials like your phone, wallet, and passport in a sling purse across your front where pickpockets are less likely to steal them. Next, always bring snacks and an empty water bottle to use while waiting at the departure gate. Bring gum because chewing it helps with ear popping during takeoff and landing. Nana has been on mission trips worldwide, so she knows what she's talking about.

Next, I went to check on Liam. His pack looked like it might burst, but it was lumpy. I had a bad feeling about this. It seemed like he packed rocks instead of clothes.

"What's in the backpack, Liam?

"Nunya."

"Open the backpack, Liam."

"No, I don't need your help; I can pack my stuff by myself."

"Look, Nana told me to check your pack to make sure you had all the essentials, like clothes."

Liam crossed his arms and glared at me. "Get outta my room."

I pretended to walk away, then turned, and grabbed his pack, snatching it right out of his hands. I held it up over his head as he jumped up and down, trying to get back. I unzipped it, and cars, books, toys, and his whip came flying out—no clothes.

"Stop! Leave me alone," Liam yelled.

"Look, dummy, we'll be gone for two weeks, and you didn't pack any clothes!"

"Did so!" he yelled as he pulled a pair of underwear from his pocket.

I rolled my eyes. "One pair of drawers is not going to do it. Now, come on, let's repack this."

He glared at me, stomped to his bed, and flopped down. "Fine. But I wanna take some toys, too, and my whip."

"Your whip? No, the airlines might think that's a weapon and arrest you."

"If I'm going on a great adventure, I need my whip and hat like Bill Bates and Indiana Jones."

I sighed. "Fine, but we'll have to put it at the bottom of your pack and not pull it out until we get to Egypt. Maybe they'll think it's a belt." Liam beamed brightly.

I marched over to his chest of drawers, pulled clothes out, and tossed them on the bed. "Come on, dude, pick out your favorites, and let's get on with this." Liam sifted through them as I sat beside him, folding and stuffing them into his pack.

We packed his whip on the bottom, a week's worth of clothes, a second pair of shoes, a sweatshirt, a comb, a toothbrush, toothpaste, and some toys. "Okay, this is better, and you still have room to fit in some comics and your Nintendo."

"Great, thanks, now get out!"

"Brat," I muttered. "I shoulda let you wander around in dirty clothes for two weeks, but I didn't wanna smell your stink. Honestly, only one pair of drawers."

"You know I don't need underwear; I can go commando."

"Eww, no, that's gross."

Liam laughed and ran outside to play.

"Boys are disgusting," I muttered to myself.

Finally, the time came to go to the airport. Nana called us downstairs, lined us up by the door, and read off her list. "Okay, do I have the plane tickets and passports?" She checked her purse. "Yep, they're here. Do we all have a backpack with clothes and other necessities?"

I nodded, while Liam jumped to attention and barked, "Ma'am, yes, ma'am." I just rolled my eyes.

"Does everybody have an empty reusable water bottle, plugs for electronics, extra batteries, chargers, snacks, gum, tissues, sunglasses, hats, and hand sanitizer?"

I nodded while Liam jumped to attention again and barked, "Ma'am, yes, ma'am."

"Would you please stop that?" I snapped at Liam.

Nana was digging in her purse. "Keys, yes; wallet, yes; cash, yes; credit cards, yes; phone, yes. Cara, do you have your phone?"

I rolled my eyes. As if I would forget my phone. "Yes, Nana, can we go now? The Uber is going to be here any minute."

"Okay, is everybody ready?"

"Ma'am, yes, ma'am."

"That's it! One more time, Liam and I'll smack you upside the head." Liam giggled.

"Cara, be patient; he's just excited to go on a great adventure."

"Nana, please don't say that; it just encourages him to irritate the snot out of me."

Nana snickered.

"It's not funny!"

Nana leaned over and whispered to me, "Honey, today's life lesson is that little brothers never listen to or obey their older sisters, but you've gotta love them anyway."

I folded my arms across my chest and snorted in disgust. I hated it when she was right.

Nana straightened up and tried to appear stern, but I could see the smile creeping around her mouth. I rolled my eyes.

There was a knock at the door. My best friend Rachel, her mom, and Danny, her brother, were here to pick up the house keys. They would watch the house and water the plants while we were away.

"Hey, girl, I see you're ready to go. Man, I wish I could go with you," Rachel told me.

"Yes, everyone in the neighborhood is jealous of you, Mary," Rachel's mom told Nana. "Anyway, I'm here for the house keys. Show me which plants you want me to water while you're gone, and where should I drop off the mail?"

Nana walked away with Rachel's mom, while Rachel and I chatted, and Liam and Danny sat on the stoop.

"Are you gonna ride camels in Egypt?" Danny asked Liam.

"I dunno, but I hope so," Liam replied.

"What happens if you find a mummy?"

"I'm gonna try and find one; that would be awesome. It would be a great adventure!"

"But what if it has a curse or something?"

"I ain't afraid of no curse. I'll have my whip. Any monsters come near me, and they'll feel the sting of my whip like you did."

Danny nodded. "Cool, cool. That should work."

I rolled my eyes, and Rachel smiled.

"So, promise you'll send me pics and text me on WhatsApp if anything exciting happens," she said.

"I promise."

The Uber pulled up to the house, and the driver beeped the horn. We all ran outside, piled in, waved goodbye to our friends, and off we went to Newport News International Airport. We flew straight to New York to catch a flight to our first stop in England. On the airplane, we were cramped in the budget seats.

When we arrived in New York, Nana upgraded us to business class.

"My legs and my butt are sore," she whispered. "I need more room than those cheap seats provide."

Nana jokes that she inherited the "Cullen butt." Her maiden name was Cullen, and all the women in her family had large butts, just like hers. Her favorite outfits are stretch pants and sweatshirts because they are comfortable.

Unlike Sir Mix-a-Lot, I don't like big butts, so I'm

determined not to inherit the Cullen butt. Luckily, so far, I have my dad's family butt, which is tiny. Like Nana, I love sweatshirts but prefer jeans and a T-shirt; stretch pants felt a little too old-ladyish.

Soon, we boarded the airplane. Once I settled into my seat, I pulled out my journal and wrote about the business-class seats. Boy, were they nicer than the others.

Dear Journal,

I am finally on my way to Egypt, and in business-class seats, no less. Thanks, Nana, for the upgrade! The seats and legroom are so much roomier. This is awesome. I can't wait to see my dad.

I stopped writing and took a quick peek out the window, thinking how lucky I was not to have to sit near Liam for the seven-hour trip to England. I felt terrible for Nana because she volunteered to sit beside him and give me a break.

I was putting my journal away and stuffing my bag under the seat in front of me when someone plopped down next to me. I turned to look. Next to me was the most gorgeous guy, a little older than me, with wavy brown hair, brown eyes, and a smile that could melt your socks. My heart raced, my hands started to sweat, and I gulped in some air, causing me to cough like an idiot.

"Are you alright?"

I covered my mouth as I tried to recover and nodded. "Yeah, sure..." Cough, cough. "I'm fine..." Cough, cough.

"My name is Benjamin, Ben for short. What's your name?"

"I'm, um, I'm Cara. Cara for short," I babbled. *Great. What a nitwit I am.* I managed to smile a weak smile.

He laughed. "Have you ever been to England?"

"No, this is my first trip across the ocean."

Just then, I heard Liam scream. I couldn't see what was happening, so I jumped up and said, "Ben, I need to get out to the aisle; my little brother just screamed, and I have to see if everything is okay."

Ben jumped up and moved aside so I could get out. I pushed my way through the crowd of passengers, trying to reach their seats while calling out, "Liam? Nana? Where are you guys? Is everything okay?"

They were several rows ahead of me, and when I finally reached them, Liam was standing in his seat, leaning over to shake hands with the man in front of him. He was babbling to the poor guy, almost hysterical. I turned to look at the man and realized it was Bill Bates from our favorite TV show. My mouth dropped open. I couldn't breathe. I looked at Nana in astonishment, pointing at Mr. Bates.

Liam jumped up and down in his seat. "Cara, it's Bill Bates! He's right here! He's my hero. That's my sister, and this is my grandma, Nana, and I want to go on an adventure with you—find dinosaur bones or pirate treasure..."

Nana looked at me and said, "Yep, it's everyone's favorite adventurer, Mr. Bill Bates. Close your mouth, honey, and say hi."

"Hi," I squeaked. Mr. Bates extended his hand for me to shake. I hesitantly took it and gave it a weak shake, trying not to faint.

He smiled and said, "Good to meet you."

There he was in person, taller than I had envisioned. His hair and beard were a reddish-brown with hints of gray. Freckles dotted his face, and he wore his signature untucked shirt, cargo pants, and ever-present fedora. It felt like meeting Indiana Jones.

People began to stare. "Liam, sit down and stop making such a fuss," Nana said, tugging at his pant leg.

Mr. Bates chuckled. "Good to meet you all. Maybe we can go on an adventure when you're older, but for now, you're a bit too young, buddy."

"But I want to go with you now," Liam insisted.

I chimed in. "Liam, you can't go now. We're going to see Dad, remember?"

Liam sighed. "Okay, but maybe we can go after that," he said hopefully.

Mr. Bates winked at him. "We'll see, little buddy, we'll see. For now, you'd better sit down and buckle up. It looks like they're closing the outside doors."

Liam obediently sat down and buckled up. Man, I'd really like to know how he does that; Liam never listens to me.

I heard someone behind me say, "Oh, brother." When I turned around, Ben rolled his eyes so far back in his head that I thought they might fall to the floor. He turned and marched back to his seat.

"Sorry about that," I told Mr. Bates, but he just smiled and shrugged.

I returned to my seat next to Ben. "That was my annoying little brother, Liam, and my grandmother, Nana. We're heading to Egypt to see my dad, with a layover in England."

Ben sighed and said, "Yeah, we're heading to Egypt too. And that was my dad."

My eyes widened in surprise. "THAT was your dad? Your last name is Bates?" He nodded. "So, you're going on an adventure with him?"

"Yes, and his squad of photographers, sound guys, drone operators, etc. It's not a vacay; it's work, and I barely get to see him."

"Wow, I'm sorry. I know what you mean. My dad's on deployment with the navy. I haven't seen him for six months except through Zoom. The three of us are on our way to spend time with him. Those two up there are my squad, not quite as big as yours."

We both smiled. "Well, at least I have someone cute to talk to on the long flight to England," he said with a wink. I could feel my face turning bright red.

I quickly turned to look out the window. "Well, look at that, we're moving," I muttered. *He thinks I'm cute! OMG.* My heart raced, and my palms were sweaty again. I shoved my hands under my thighs to hide them.

"So, um, are you and your dad and his squad going to Giza to see the pyramids?" I asked.

"No, but we'll be near them; we're going to the pyramids of Dahshur."

"What are you going to do there?"

He shrugged. "I dunno, probably die of boredom."

"What? No, don't say that. It's the pyramids, one of the Seven Wonders of the World. You'll get to walk where the pharaohs walked and uncover ancient artifacts. Man, I envy you."

"I'm excited about seeing all the sites, but archaeology isn't my thing; it's my dad's thing. It can be hard, dirty work digging up those artifacts. I'd rather be on my surfboard, catching some waves, walking on the beach, collecting shells, deep-sea diving, or whale watching. I want to be a marine biologist. I start college at Boston U this fall."

Crap, he's in college. I'm just starting tenth grade. "Well, um, that's cool. Yeah, I'm planning to be a writer. I'll probably get my degree in journalism. Eventually, I want to write books, but I also like the idea of writing for a major publication."

"Which college will you be attending?"

Think, Cara, think. "Um, I, uh, I've got options, but I haven't chosen one yet." *Is avoiding the truth the same as lying? Just tell him you're in high school!* As a follower of Jesus, I tried never to lie. I could feel the Holy Spirit nudging me to do the right thing and admit I was in high school.

"Well, you better hurry; they fill up quickly."

I nodded and turned back to the window. *Crap, I know better than to lie; it always comes back to bite me.* But he had to be at least three years older than me. He would think of me as a little kid when I wanted him to see me as an equal.

"Looks like we're taking off now," I said. "Want some gum? Nana says it'll help keep your ears from popping as the plane rises."

He smiled and took a piece of gum. We leaned back and waited for the plane to reach cruising altitude before trying to talk over the engine noise. Soon, the plane leveled off, and the engines settled into a quieter hum.

The seatbelt sign turned off, and we heard, "You are now free to move about the cabin. For your safety, when seated, please keep your seatbelt buckled. Thank you."

Ben and I continued chatting about books, movies, TV shows, and other stuff. We had a lot in common. We both liked biographies and superhero movies. We watched the same TV series. We pulled out our phones and compared our favorite YouTube videos, laughing until we cried.

We were interrupted as Liam ran down the aisle and stopped beside us.

"Who are you?" he asked Ben.

"I'm Ben, and you must be Liam."

"Yeah, that's me. I need to speak to my sister. Cara, can you come with me to the back?"

I rolled my eyes. "Can't you manage the toilet by yourself?"

"Just come with me," Liam hissed through gritted teeth.

"Fine!" I got up and apologized as I stepped over Ben to get to the aisle. Even at thirty thousand feet, I couldn't escape my little brother. Ben watched them leave, shaking his head and laughing.

Liam and I reached the back of the plane near the bathroom. I opened one of the stall doors and gestured for Liam to go in.

"No, I don't have to go; I just wanted to talk to you alone."

I looked at the ceiling and huffed. "Fine, what do you want?"

"I want you to help me go on an adventure with Mr. Bates."

"No, didn't you hear him? He said you're too little. The man doesn't even know you. Why would he let you go with him? Forget it; I'm not asking him to take you."

"I don't want you to ask him anything. I want you to help me sneak into his truck, stuff me in one of his bags, or hide me in the trunk of his car."

My mouth fell open. "You have lost your mind. Go sit down by Nana and behave yourself!"

Liam growled and stomped back to his seat. "You make me so mad!" he yelled over his shoulder.

Several people glanced at me. I shrugged and smiled, twirling my finger around my temple to indicate that Liam was crazy, and then quickly marched back to my seat.

When I returned, Ben asked, "Is everything okay with Liam? I thought I saw steam coming out of the top of his head when he stomped by."

"Yeah, he's just being his bratty self. Man, he's so stubborn. He gets a wild idea for a misadventure and won't let it go."

"Misadventure?"

"That's what we call his crazy wild outings to find something. He never says what he is looking for, but he takes off through the mall, the cornfield, or down the street, and we can't find him. When we finally do find him, he's usually mixed up in something he shouldn't be, and it's a mess. This time, he asked me to stuff him in your dad's trunk so he could go with you guys to Dahshur."

Ben laughed heartily. "That's fantastic! I love this kid."

"You may laugh now, but you'd better check your car trunk and luggage for a stowaway before leaving for Dahshur," I said.

He laughed again. His laughter was delightful, sending a thrill down my spine. I wondered if I was falling for Ben. Could a person fall in love so quickly? How do you know when you are in love anyway?

Chapter 5:
Am I in Love?

I was dreaming. I was riding a camel in the desert, with the pyramids in the background, but the camel kept stumbling over rocks. Suddenly, I found myself surrounded by dark water; I was being pulled under, my heart racing, but I couldn't call out for help. Just as I was about to drown, a hand reached down and pulled me out. Before I could see who it was, I woke up.

Where was I? This wasn't my bed. Oh, right, I was on the airplane.

I looked around and realized I was leaning against Ben's shoulder. He had his arm around me and was still asleep. I slowly reached for my phone to avoid waking him. I checked the time; it was five thirty in the morning. I raised my phone, switched it to selfie mode, and captured a great shot of me leaning against Ben's arm while he slept peacefully. I carefully removed his arm and placed it on the middle armrest.

I quickly opened WhatsApp and sent the picture to Rachel, texting: *Look who sat beside me on the plane! His name is Ben—more details will come later.*

I pulled out my journal and wrote:

Dear Journal,

Wow! What a fantastic vacation already, and we are only on the airplane. I got to sit next to the most incredible guy, named Benjamin Bates. He is cute and sweet, and we have so much in common. I feel very comfortable around him. I hope this isn't the last time I see him. I pray I can hang out with him again sometime during the trip. Thank you, Jesus, for such a wonderful time.

I put my journal away and gently stepped over Ben to reach the aisle. He was still asleep when I trotted back from the bathroom. I went to check on Liam and Nana.

As Cara passed Ben, he opened one eye and watched her walk away down the aisle toward her family. "Boy, I wish she were coming to Boston U this fall," he muttered to himself before closing his eyes to go back to sleep.

Liam was stretched out with his head in Nana's lap, fast asleep, while Nana snored loudly. I felt embarrassed because Mr. Bates was awake and working on his laptop.

"Mr. Bates," I whispered, "I'm so sorry my grandmother is keeping you awake."

He lifted his head from his screen. "Huh? Oh, no, they aren't bothering me; I'm always up this early. You're Cara, right?"

I nodded.

"Here, sit down, talk to me." He moved his papers from the seat beside him and stuffed them into his pack near his feet.

"No one is sitting here?" I asked.

"No, I always buy an extra seat to stretch out and work or sleep."

Wow, that sounded wise. I felt nervous about talking to one of my heroes. I wondered if I could take a selfie with him and add it to my journal, but I was too shy to ask.

"Your grandmother is sweet," said Mr. Bates. "She told me all about her life lessons."

I rolled my eyes. "Yes, it's annoying, but some of them are actually helpful. I'm sitting next to your son, Ben. He tells me you're going to Dahshur on a dig. My dad booked us a tour of the pyramids in Giza."

"Yeah, all the tourists go there, but the pyramids in Dahshur are incredible and older than those in

Giza. Your family should make the time to visit them, too. Did Ben seem excited when you talked to him?"

I couldn't tell him that Ben expected to be bored and would rather go to the beach. I didn't want to disappoint his dad with the truth that archaeology wasn't what he wanted to pursue in life, but I also didn't want to lie again. Lies are too hard to remember. "Um, he said he was looking forward to spending time with you." Not a lie. I smiled and thought, *Please don't ask for any more details.*

He smiled and nodded. "Your grandmother and I talked, and it seems that we have a layover in London for a day. Maybe we can take you and your family out to dinner."

My eyes widened, and my heart skipped a beat. "That-that sounds great!" I stuttered. "I'm sure my grandmother wouldn't mind, and I know Liam will go bonkers." I thought I wouldn't mind spending more time with Ben, either.

"We'll go to a local pub and try their haggis," he said.

"What's haggis?"

"It's a meat dish traditionally made from a sheep's heart, liver, and lungs, cooked in the sheep's stomach," he grinned.

I felt nauseous at the thought of eating that, and it must have shown on my face because he burst out laughing. "Just kidding, you don't have to eat that.

Besides, it's a Scottish dish. But I had it once, and it wasn't bad."

"If it has liver in it, I'm not eating it," I said. "How about some fish and chips instead?"

"You got it, kid."

"Well, I'll let you get back to your work. Um, before I go, could I get a selfie with you?" My heart exploded in my chest, and my hands shook when I asked him for a photo.

He smiled, saying, "Sure, no problem." My hands were still shaky, but I pulled my phone from my pocket and snapped a selfie with Bill Bates. I took several, hoping at least one wouldn't be blurry. Then I smiled and returned to my seat.

On my way back, I texted Rachel the picture along with the message: *This is Ben's dad, and yes, that's Bill Bates!*

When I arrived, Ben was awake. He stretched as I took my seat. "Good morning. So, you slept well last night," he said.

"What do you mean?"

"I thought someone was tearing the wing off the plane, but it was just your snoring," he said with a grin.

I was mortified. I turned several shades of red and covered my mouth with my hands to keep from screaming. The most gorgeous guy in the world sat down beside me, told me I was cute, and held me while I slept—and then I ruined it by snoring like a bear! I was on the verge of tears.

He laughed loudly. "I'm kidding. Boy, you are gullible."

I punched him hard in the arm. "Not funny, punk!"

"Ow," he said. Then he laughed harder, which soon had me giggling too.

"You're your father's son. He just asked me if I wanted to eat haggis."

"Eww, do you know what that is?"

"Yes, he went on to tell me all about it. Then he said, 'Just kidding.'"

Ben grinned. "That's my dad. He loves practical jokes."

"He invited my family to dinner with all of you tonight. Maybe we can find a prank to pull on him."

"That's exactly what we should do. Then, after dinner, you and I can sneak off, grab a drink, and check out the clubs."

See, Cara, I thought, *now your lie has come back to bite you. He thinks you're old enough to drink.* "Oh, I don't know. Um, it's been a long day of travel, and I might need to crash early tonight. Besides, you're not twenty-one, are you?"

"No, I'm eighteen, which is the legal drinking age here in England. You're eighteen too, aren't you?"

Don't say it, don't lie, I heard Jesus whisper in my head. So, I avoided the questions entirely. "A lady never discusses her age, sir."

He studied my face. I glanced at the ceiling and the floor, but I avoided looking into his eyes.

"You aren't, are you? How old are you?"

"I'm too eighteen!" *You said it! You're such a liar. Shut up, self. Sorry, Jesus.*

Ben looked at me with narrowed eyes. He knew I was lying. I glanced away, sighed, and confessed.

"No, I'm not eighteen; I just turned sixteen. I'm not going to college this fall; I'll be a sophomore in high school. There, that's the truth."

"So, why lie?"

"I don't know! I wanted you to think I was older, I guess. But now you see that I'm just a stupid little kid."

"I don't think you're a stupid kid, and you definitely look older than sixteen. I like you; you're funny, smart, pretty, and a great liar."

I smiled. "Thanks. I think. I'm pretty good." Again, I felt the Holy Spirit nudging me not to take pride in being a liar. *Sorry, Jesus*, I thought in my heart. "But you have a tell."

"What's a tell?"

"It's something you do that reveals you're lying.

58

For instance, when you play poker and observe others closely, you can tell when they're bluffing. Maybe they tap their fingers, blink a lot, or have some nervous tic; that's their tell. You know they're bluffing, which is essentially lying. Your tell is that you bite your lower lip."

"Okay, good to know." So, from now on, I won't lie; if I do, I'll make sure not to bite my lip and give it away.

Liam raced down the aisle. "Cara, Mr. Bates invited us to dinner!"

"I know. I talked to him this morning while you were asleep. Ben will be there too."

Liam looked at Ben. "Why are you coming?"

"Mr. Bates is my dad."

"Really? Wow, that's great! What's he like? Do you have adventures every day? Do you have any real dinosaur bones?"

I rolled my eyes and leaned over to Ben. "Sorry, but you brought this on yourself. You should never have told him the truth. You should have said you were part of the crew."

Liam kept firing questions at a hundred miles an hour.

"If I lied to him, you would have seen my tell. That means I can no longer lie to you."

"Okay, smart guy. I'm giving my seat to Liam, so

you two can play fifty questions while I check on my Nana."

Liam didn't even take a breath. He continued firing questions as I got out of my seat and he slid in. I buckled him up and went to see Nana. When I looked back, he was leaning toward Ben, his lips flapping, and Ben was mouthing the words "Help Me!"

I snickered and kept walking. I sat down next to Nana. "Nana, you okay? Did you get any sleep?"

"No, these old bones can't sleep on airplanes."

"Well, you should tell your mouth that because you were snoring like a bull elephant." I heard Mr. Bates stifle a laugh, which made him choke and start coughing.

"I was not!"

"Just ask Mr. Bates. Didn't she snore and wake you up?"

"No." Cough, cough. "Not at all."

I quickly glanced around the seat to see if Mr. Bates had a tell when he was lying. He swiftly looked down at his papers and began shuffling them. I wasn't sure, but I thought his tell was to stop making eye contact with the person speaking and act busy instead.

The intercom buzzed as the airplane lights came on. "Good morning, passengers. We'll be serving breakfast in a few minutes. Our estimated arrival time at Heathrow is one hour and twenty minutes."

60

"I guess I'll go sit down." I went back to my seat, where Liam was still bombarding Ben with questions. "Liam, be quiet and go sit down to eat breakfast."

"Aww," he said but obediently left.

"Wow, that little guy can talk! I couldn't get a word in edgewise," Ben remarked.

"Welcome to my life," I answered.

The next few hours were chaotic. After breakfast, it didn't take long before we began our descent to Heathrow Airport. I was fortunate enough to see Windsor Castle from the air. London looked much bigger than I had expected.

Soon, the attendants hurried us off the airplane, probably relieved to see Liam go. They had spent a lot of time answering his endless questions. "Good bye. Thanks for flying with us. Have a nice day, bye now," they all muttered while forcing smiles on their faces.

"Thank you," I replied. "I'm sorry about my little brother," I whispered to one attendant. She sighed and smiled.

Liam overheard me and asked, "What did I do?"

"Just keep moving, motor mouth," I said, giving him a shove.

"Hey, cut it out."

"Liam, you ask too many questions. It annoys people." We had no extra luggage to retrieve, so we said our goodbyes to Ben and his dad and planned a time to meet for dinner. They would text us the name of the restaurant. We climbed into a cab and headed to our hotel.

"'Tis a fine bonny day, 'ere in London," remarked the cab driver.

"Your accent is Scottish," Nana said. "I have ancestors from Scotland and Ireland."

"Have you seen the Loch Ness Monster?" Liam asked. This brought a laugh from our Scottish cabbie.

"No, I ne'er saw 'er, laddie, but I keep an eye out ev'ry time I go there."

"Cool! Can I go with you? That would be an awesome adventure. Do you have a submarine we can use to see her? Maybe we can scuba dive? How about a boat? Do you—"

"Liam, enough with the questions; please leave the man alone," I exclaimed. Liam slumped back in his seat, disappointed.

The cab driver chuckled again. "Don' you worry, laddie. I'll call you next time I go." He winked at me. Liam smiled, looking excited.

Watching the city roll by from the cab was fascinating, especially since we drove on the opposite side of the road compared to what we're used to in America. As we passed, I pointed out the landmarks I recognized. "Look, there's Big Ben. Oh, over there, I see the London Eye; I would love to ride that."

Nana and Liam oohed and aahed at the

landmarks we passed. Then the cabbie pointed out other famous sites, and I joined them in the oohing and aahing until we reached our hotel. In our hotel room, Nana immediately lay down to nap.

"Nana, I didn't bring any dresses. If we're going out to dinner with Ben and his dad, I want to wear a dress. Can I go downstairs to check out the gift shop?" But she snored instead of answering me. I sighed. "Liam, I'm going downstairs to the gift shop. You stay in the room with Nana."

"No way, I wanna go too."

I rolled my eyes. "Fine, but don't touch anything. The shop is filled with expensive breakables, so be careful. And don't wander off."

I was delighted to discover a variety of lovely dresses in the gift shop. Although they were pricey, I justified purchasing one since I had birthday money upstairs in my suitcase. I knew I could charge it to my room tab, so I didn't need cash, and I could pay Dad back when he joined us. I picked a cute sundress that showcased my legs but wasn't too short to worry my Nana. I also picked up a pair of slip-on shoes since I only packed my kicks.

I gave the lady my room number, and as she rang it up, I looked around for Liam. "Liam? You ready to go?" No answer.

"Liam?" I stuffed my purchases into my backpack and then marched around the store—no Liam. I ran out to the lobby—no Liam.

"Doggone that kid! Where did he go?" I stepped out onto the street, searching right and then left. There he was, sitting on top of a red phone booth. OMG! I rushed over and yelled at him to get down.

"Why, I can see everything from here. It's like I'm sitting on the TARDIS from *Dr. Who*."

"How the heck did you get up there anyway?"

"I climbed on the trash can next to the street sign, shimmied up the sign pole, and dropped down on top of the phone booth."

"Excuse me, little man, would you mind comin' down 'ere?" It was a London police officer, with a large, rounded, black hat and a bright yellow vest marked 'police.'

Liam sighed and climbed back down the same way he went up. He stood before the police officer with his head down and his hands in his pockets, looking ashamed and drawing little circles on the sidewalk with his foot. The cop glared down at him with crossed arms. "Now, 'ere in London, we don't allow people to climb on the booths."

"Yes, sir. Sorry," muttered Liam.

The cop looked at me, smiled, and winked. "Do you know what we do to criminals 'ere in London?"

Liam looked up at him, then at me. "No sir."

"Why we lock 'em in the tower of London and only feed 'em bread and water. Now you don't wanna do that, do ya?" Liam shook his head no. "Alright then, off you go with your sister, and don't be climbin' on the booths anymore." Liam nodded, and we walked away.

"Liam, you need to learn to control your misadventure nature. I don't want to have to bail you out of jail."

"Okay."

Later that evening, we all gathered with the Bates group and sat down to enjoy a lovely dinner. Ben was seated next to me.

"You look beautiful. I love your dress."

I felt myself blush. "Thanks."

We were all at a large table elegantly adorned with a white linen tablecloth and napkins, stunning cream china plates, and green glass goblets filled with sparkling water. The waiters brought us plates piled high with beef, roasted potatoes, and carrots, smothered in rich gravy, plus Yorkshire pudding on the side. It was so delicious that I contemplated staying in London and skipping Egypt entirely just to indulge in more English cooking.

Liam sat next to Mr. Bates and began asking questions. Mr. Bates held up a hand. "Whoa! How about instead of questions, I share a story about one of my adventures?"

Liam grinned and nodded.

Mr. Bates shared exciting stories of his travel adventures while we ate. We laughed until we cried.

"He really has had an incredible life," I whispered to Ben.

Ben sighed. "Yeah, I just wish more of his tales included me. My parents divorced when I was young. Mom wouldn't let me go with him. She wanted me to have a regular home life and stay in school, but I longed to be with my dad."

"I understand. I wish my dad would leave the navy and stay with us. But it's not too late; you can still spend time with him."

"Maybe. We'll see." He leaned in closely and whispered in my ear, "How about you and I create some adventures of our own? I can pick you up at your hotel around eleven tonight, and we'll go clubbing."

His breath warmed my neck, sending shivers down my spine and causing my heart to race. I knew I shouldn't go, but I really wanted to. If Liam could take misadventures all the time and get away with them, maybe I should give it a shot, too.

"As long as my grandmother and Liam are asleep, I can sneak out. But we can't stay out too late."

Ben winked. "Now, about that prank on my dad. John, one of the camera guys, will be hiding behind the suit of armor in the hall down there." Ben pointed toward the back of the room. "Mike, the drone operator, will tell a story about the armor being haunted. I've paid the waiter to inform my dad that there's a phone call for him on the landline next to the suit of armor. When he goes to answer, I'll film it with my phone.

When my dad gets near the suit, John will move the armor's arms and moan. It's going to freak my dad out. I hope to capture him screaming like a little girl."

"Oh, that's so mean! You know he'll have to get back at you, right?"

Ben nodded and grinned widely.

Mike captured everyone's attention. "I just learned from one of the waiters that the suit of armor over there is haunted. Sometimes, you can actually see its arms move, and it makes ghostly moaning sounds at night. Do you want to hear the story?" Everyone nodded or eagerly said yes, so Mike shared a tale of his own invention about a knight who perished on the battlefield but was forever cursed to wander the earth after death.

A few minutes later, the waiter approached the table and said, "Mr. Bates, there's a call for you on the landline in the hall by the suit of armor."

Bill looked at the waiter and stood up. "Are you sure they want to speak to me?" he asked the waiter.

"Aye, they do," the waiter replied.

I could tell that Mr. Bates felt uncertain about this. He scanned the table and noticed that some of his crew were missing. He glanced at his son, but Ben pretended to show me something on his phone. Bill shrugged and walked down the hall toward the phone.

The phone closest to the armor was off the hook, so Bill picked it up and said, "Hello, this is Bill Bates."

The arms of the armor began to move, and a moan escaped from behind it. Instead of screaming, Mr. Bates muttered into the phone, "What? I can't hear you. The armor is moaning. What? Oh, okay." He handed the phone to the armor. "It's for you; your mummy's calling."

I burst into laughter as Ben's mouth dropped open. He kept filming his dad, who hung up the wall phone, walked over to Ben, and said, "Son, you've gotta do better than that if you want to freak me out." Then he grinned and returned to the table. Ben shut off his phone and rolled his eyes.

On the way back to the hotel, Ben was all I could think about. Liam dozed off in the cab, leaning against Nana.

"So, Ben is cute, isn't he?" Nana remarked.

I sighed. "Yeah, he is. Nana, do you have a life lesson about how to tell if you're in love?"

"Well, there are many ways to tell if you're attracted to someone. For example, you can't stop thinking about them, your hands get sweaty when they're nearby, seeing them makes your heart race, and you might become clumsy or start stuttering. However, to know if it's true love, you need to spend time with them and understand how they think and behave. Explore their moral character and determine if it aligns with your own. The Bible says, 'Don't be unequally yoked.'"

"What does that mean?"

"It refers to two oxen yoked together to plow a field. The oxen must be similar in size and strength to work together effectively and create straight rows for the crops. For a good marriage, the husband and wife must pull together during life's difficulties. So, like the oxen, they need to be in harmony and agree with each other. Do you believe you're in love with Ben?"

"I don't know."

"Well, I don't think you can truly know in just one day, and I doubt you'll see him again since he's leaving tomorrow. Maybe you two can try a long-distance relationship, like using Facebook or Whats Nap or something."

I rolled my eyes. "No one my age uses Facebook, Nana, and it's WhatsApp, not nap."

"Sorry, I can't keep up with all the latest tech stuff. But you can still stay in touch with Ben, remain friends, and see where it goes from there."

Why was she always right? It was so annoying.

Chapter 6:
A Hidden Passage

Back at the hotel, I carried Liam inside and laid him on the bed. I took off his shoes and covered him with the blanket. He never woke up. Nana got ready for bed, and I grabbed my journal to write.

"Aren't you coming to bed?"

"Sure, I just want to finish writing about my day."

Nana shrugged. "Okay, good night." Within three minutes, she was asleep. I had never seen anyone fall asleep as quickly as she did. Soon, she and Liam were snoring away.

Dear Journal,

My heart is in my throat as I wait for Nana to fall asleep. I have never snuck out before, and it feels a lot like lying. I hope she doesn't wake up when I come back. I have to be very

*quiet. I will leave a note on the table telling
Nana I'm with Ben in case something goes
wrong.*

I felt uneasy, as if Jesus were watching me make
a bad choice. I ignored the feeling and checked my
phone: 10:50 p.m. Okay, if I was going to do this, I had
to sneak out now. I tucked my phone and the room
key into my pockets, grabbed my jacket, and tiptoed
toward the door.

My heart raced as I slowly opened the door.
It creaked. Oh wow, that was loud. I turned, but
everyone was snoring, so I continued. Soon, I found
myself in the elevator, heading to the lobby. I let out
a deep breath.

I scanned the lobby and quickly spotted Ben by
the door, waiting patiently. He smiled when he saw
me. "I wasn't sure you'd come."

"I had to wait until everyone started snoring."

"I had it easier. My dad and the crew had a
late-night meeting to plan the week and discuss the
filming. I just walked out the door. No one noticed.
Anyway, I am taking you to a special place tonight.
Since you are not eighteen, we can't get into a lot of
the clubs, but my mom has a friend who owns one
where they have a DJ. I'm sure we can get in there
with no problem."

Ben hailed a cab, and we were off. We instructed
the driver on where to take us. As we entered the club,
loud music was thumping away. The whole building

72

shook. People were dancing and drinking; the noise was deafening.

The guy at the door looked at us, "Can I see your ID, please?" he asked.

Ben and I took out our passports. "The name's Ben Bates, my mom is Sarah Langston Gates, a friend of the owner. Please tell Mr. Hennison we're here."

The man growled and walked off to inform his boss, nodding to someone behind the door. Instantly, another giant stood in his place, blocking the door. This guy was even scarier than the last. He towered over us, glaring. We actually took a step back and waited.

A few minutes passed, and a middle-aged man came walking over, grinning ear to ear, with the doorman right behind him.

"Ben? Is that you?" He asked.

"Hi, Mr. Hennison," Ben said as he reached out to shake the man's hand.

"Look how you've grown. Wow, time flies. How's your mother? Is she here?" Mr. Hennison grabbed Ben's hand and shook it up and down vigorously.

"No, my mom is still in the US. I'm here with my dad. But I'd like you to meet my friend, Cara."

"Welcome, Cara." Mr. Hennison waved us in. "Come in, enjoy yourselves. I have business to attend to, but I will try and chat with you later. Bob, show them to my reserved table."

The bouncer, Bob, led us through the crowd to a small table in the back. As we pushed our way through the crowd, I yelled to Ben, "This is my first club experience."

"What?"

"This is my first club experience," I shouted louder.

Ben nodded. "Do you want a drink?"

"What?"

"Do you want a drink?" Ben shouted above the noise.

I nodded. "Is it always this loud?" I yelled.

Ben nodded. "Do you want a beer?"

"What?"

"Do you want a beer?" He said louder.

"Sure, a root beer would be fine, thanks."

"What?"

I nodded and pointed to the bartender since it was impossible to communicate over the noise. I sat down and looked around while Ben went for our drinks.

Soon, he returned with two glasses of dark liquid, which I thought was root beer. Ben took a big swig and wiped his mouth with the back of his hand.

I took a large gulp of the dark liquid and immediately started coughing and choking. Not root beer!

Crap, that stuff was nasty. Why would anyone want to drink that swill?

"Are you alright?"

I nodded. "Went down the wrong pipe," I managed to choke out. "What kind of root beer is this?"

He laughed. "It's not root beer; it's English ale or their version of beer."

"Smooth," I said, holding up the glass. I didn't mention that I thought the beer was nasty. Instead, I decided to hold the glass and pretend I enjoyed it. I'd raise it to my lips and act like I was swallowing occasionally, but I didn't want it in my mouth anymore. So, my first sip of alcohol. Great, just one more nail in my coffin if my dad found out.

The music was good. My feet were tapping as I leaned against the table.

"You wanna dance?" Ben asked.

I nodded, and we squeezed our way onto the dance floor, jumping and moving to the music. Ben was a pretty good dancer. Everyone laughed, clapped, and had a great time until the song came to an end. The next song was slow, and people started pairing off. Ben took my hand and pulled me close. We swayed to the music, and I felt safe and warm in his arms. I leaned against his chest and sighed, wishing this moment would last forever.

Finally, the music ended, and we returned to our table. The DJ took a break, making it quieter and allowing us to talk in normal voices. Aside from the ringing in my ears, it was a magical evening.

Mr. Hennison came back and stood beside us to chat. "So, why are you in London, Ben?"

"I'm with my dad and his crew. They will be filming at a new dig site near the pyramids at Dahshur," Ben said.

"How exciting, when do you leave for Egypt?"

"We leave tomorrow," Ben replied.

"Well, just in case you are still in town, here's a more age-appropriate event you can attend tomorrow," he said as he hastily scribbled an address on a napkin.

"Thanks, Mr. Hennison, and I'll be sure and tell my mom you said hi." Ben remarked as he took the napkin.

Ben's phone beeped with a text. "Crap, it's my dad. He's looking for me."

Ben's Dad: *Where are you?*

Ben: *I took a walk. Not far. Be back soon.*

I watched him as he texted and noticed his tell. "Aha, I see your tell. Now I'll know when you're lying to me."

"What? No way."

"Yes, when you lie, you wrinkle your nose."

Ben rolled his eyes. "Okay, you got me. My dad

says I do that, too. Come on, I'll take you back to your hotel."

We laughed as we got into the cab. Ben gave the driver the address, looked at me, and asked, "Did you have a good time?"

"It was the best." Then he leaned over and kissed me. It was a long, passionate kiss that made me feel things I had never experienced, and I panicked, pushing him away.

"Did I do something wrong?"

"No, no, that was, um, wonderful. But unexpected." I was panting, trying to catch my breath.

"Sorry. I forgot you are younger than me." He leaned back in his seat and was quiet for the rest of the ride.

After a few minutes, I tentatively reached over and touched his hand. He smiled and interlaced his fingers with mine. We held hands all the way to the hotel, and as we walked through the lobby and up the elevator, we finally stopped at my hotel room door.

"Good night," Ben said, kissing me on the cheek.

"Good night." I watched him until the elevator doors shut, then quietly opened my door with the key. I tiptoed into the room, using my phone for light to find my pajamas and quickly change. Just as I was ready to slide into bed, my phone beeped, indicating I had a text.

It was Rachel. *Are you kidding me? What a hottie!*

Give me details, NOW!

I had to stifle a laugh. I spent the next thirty minutes texting Rachel about Ben, his dad, and all the exciting things that had happened so far.

Finally, we signed off, and I carefully slid into bed with Nana. No one woke up. I smiled as I realized I had gotten away with my night out on the town. My misadventure was a success! I went to sleep thinking about Ben and that kiss.

###

Early the next day, I got a text from the airline:

We regret to inform you that your flight has been delayed due to a severe sandstorm in Cairo. We have rebooked your flight for tomorrow at 11:00 a.m.

"Hey, Nana, we should call the hotel front desk and see if we can stay another night here. The airline says our flight is delayed until tomorrow."

"Did they say why?"

"Would you believe it's because of a sandstorm?"

"Okay, I'll call your dad and let him know."

"A sandstorm? Wow, can we see it?" asked Liam.

"No, Liam, we're in England. By the time we get to Egypt, the storm will be over. Hey, I'm going to text Ben and see if they're delayed too."

Me: *Hey, our flight is delayed. How about yours?*

Ben: *Yeah, we're delayed too. Dad decided to see some sights, including a medieval castle. Wanna tag along? We can meet in the lobby in half an hour.*

Me: *Yes, see you then.*

Liam, Nana, and I packed the things we would need for the day into our backpacks and headed downstairs for breakfast.

Liam was so excited. "This is my dream come true—a great adventure with Bill Bates. Do you think we'll see a dragon? Or maybe knights in armor? Will we meet a king?"

I rolled my eyes. It would be a long day filled with endless questions from Liam, but at least I'd be with Ben. I sighed.

"Well, it looks like you have another opportunity to determine if you're in love with Ben or not," Nana whispered in my ear. I just sighed.

After breakfast, we waited in the hotel foyer. Soon, Ben arrived and escorted us to the bus they had hired for the day.

Ben acted as our tour guide, complete with a fake English accent.

"Good day, guv'nor. 'Ow about poppin' on this bus so we can get started. We be off to see the castle of Laird Cornwallis of the Glenns or some other high and mighty gent."

We all laughed.

Liam ran to the seat next to Mr. Bates and plopped down next to him. "Where are we going, Mr. Bates?"

"Well, I have some special places to visit today. First, we'll stop at a real castle to join a medieval festival. Then, we'll tour the Globe Theatre to stand on stage and re-enact some of Shakespeare's plays. My film crew plans to use some of the footage in an upcoming episode. Would you like to be a part of that, Liam?"

"Oh, boy, would I!"

I looked at Ben. "Seriously? We're going to be in an upcoming episode of *Exploring the Ancients*?"

He smiled. "Yeah, Dad loves to include some shots of old England and some acting. His ancestors are from Scotland, which explains the red hair."

We traveled to Warwick Castle, where a medieval festival featured jousting and sword fighting tournaments. Medieval craftsmen sold wares, food vendors sold food, and there was singing and dancing. There was even a tent where costumes could be rented for the day.

Soon, we were trying on costumes. I chose a beautiful medieval dress with long, flowing sleeves and a small hat adorned with a silky, flowing veil. I felt like a princess. Nana was still in her sweatpants. "Nana, aren't you going to change into a costume?"

"No, honey. Today's life lesson: Know your limits.

I'm pretty sure there aren't any dresses here that would fit my big behind. I think I'll just watch and take pictures. But you look beautiful. Let me get a picture of you."

Nana snapped several pictures while I posed.

We left the women's dressing room to find all the boys ready to go. Mr. Bates and several of his crew were stomping around in armor. One was dressed like a jester, and Liam wore a child's tunic.

"This feels like a dress," he complained.

Nana was snapping his picture. "It's not a dress; it's a tunic. Look, the knights are wearing them over their armor."

"I wanna wear armor too!"

"Sorry, buddy. They don't have any in your size, but you can be my squire," said Mr. Bates.

"What's a squire?"

As a squire, one has an important job. He is a knight in training. He follows the knight everywhere and learns how to be a knight by assisting with tasks such as holding his sword or helmet, taking care of the knight's horse, and other duties. Do you think you can handle the job?"

"Oh, boy. Yeah, I'd love to be your squire!"

"Great. Here," Mr. Bates said, handing Liam his helmet. "Start by hanging onto this."

Liam grabbed the heavy object and immediately

sank onto one knee under its weight. He struggled to rise while holding the helmet and muttered, "No problem. I got it. Ugh."

I heard a few snickers from the other adults and covered my mouth to keep from laughing out loud. Turning around so Liam wouldn't see me smile, I noticed Ben staring at me. My heart skipped a beat. He looked so handsome in his tunic and tights, which were a brilliant blue with purple and gold trim. A small sword hung at his waist. He looked like Prince Charming.

OMG, don't pass out! I thought to myself.

"Wow, you look great," he said to me.

Breathe, Cara, breathe. "Um, th-thanks, um, so do you," I stuttered.

Then we just stood there, staring at each other for an awkward amount of time. In the meantime, Nana was snapping our picture and giggling.

Finally, one of the film crew members, dressed like a jester, cleared his throat and broke the silence. "Um, if you two are done drooling over each other, we need to move on with our day." Some of the others snickered or laughed out loud. How embarrassing! I turned away from Ben, my cheeks flushed with embarrassment. Ben turned and glared at the person who spoke.

"Okay, we'll start filming over at the jousting ring. Does anyone want to try their hand at jousting?" asked Bill.

"Me, me, I do!" Liam yelled.

"I was joking, buddy; you must be trained to do this. It's very dangerous."

"What is jousting anyway?"

"You charge at your opponent on horseback with a lance or spear in hand while they do the same. You collide at full speed until one of you is thrown off their horse. The winner remains seated on their horse."

Liam grimaced. "That sounds awful."

Bill laughed. "Yeah, it's pretty harsh. How about we watch them and then check out the sword fighting?" Bill instructed the film crew to follow and capture everything. Liam struggled to keep up while carrying Bill's helmet.

Bill turned back and asked, "You doing okay, Liam?" Liam nodded.

After cheering for the jousters for a few minutes, we made our way to the sword fighting, and Bill was invited to try it. Even Liam was allowed to join in.

The first up was Liam. He wore cardboard armor, a plastic helmet, and carried a cardboard tube as a makeshift sword. Another boy his age was similarly dressed, and they were taught how to fight with swords. The two enjoyed jabbing at each other, and the competition was declared a tie. After this, Liam and Nana ran off to find the demonstrations on falconry and armor-making and to watch the sword swallower.

Bill was next. "Okay, let's have fun with this. Can I get three chairs, some paper, and magic markers? I have a plan." A staff member from the castle brought the items over. Ben, the jester, and I sat in the chairs, put on dark sunglasses, and held the papers in our laps. "Okay, you three are the tournament judges, like in the Olympics. Give each of us knights a score from zero to ten. May the best man win."

The other crew members and spectators gathered around to watch the scene. Bill proceeded to gear up for the sword fight. He was placed in the ring with another man of similar height and weight. Both were in real armor and wielded real swords.

Feeling a little nervous, Bill turned to the crowd and opened with a riddle. "Say, what do you call a knight who leaves in the middle of a fight?" No one answered.

"Sir Render. Get it? Anybody? Anybody?"

Crickets. Someone moaned, another groaned, eyes rolled, and Ben said, "No, just no."

"Y'all are no fun," Bill muttered.

Bill turned to face his opponent. At first, he could barely move in all the armor, and as he stumbled around, everyone chuckled. Then, he lifted the heavy sword and swung it over his head, causing the momentum and weight to shift, making him fall back onto the grass. This provoked loud laughter, applause, and cheers from the crowd. Meanwhile, the other swordsman waited patiently.

Bill struggled to get up and into position once more. Finally, with a sword in hand, he faced his opponent, prepared to fight. The referee signaled for them to begin, and the other man lunged at Bill, who turned and ran, dropping his sword. The other man waited. Bill paused, bent over at the waist, and took several deep breaths. The referee asked if he was ready; Bill nodded and retrieved his sword.

Once again, the referee signaled to start, and the man lunged at Bill anew. Bill swung his sword wildly but managed to evade the man's advances. He yelled, prompting the crowd to cheer and laugh until his sword got knocked from his hands. He grabbed it again and ran away from his opponent, then turned to fight once more. The crowd loved it!

The two opponents circled the enclosure, swords swinging, and clashing loudly only on the rare occasions when they made contact. The heavy armor soon began to wear Bill down, prompting him to raise his hands in surrender. The other man raised his sword, strutting around the ring like a champion amid the crowd's cheers.

Bill marched over to us at our chairs and took off his helmet. His head was sweaty, his hair stuck to his scalp, and he was huffing and puffing.

"So, how'd I do? What's the score?" he asked breathlessly.

The crew filmed the exchange as we sat expressionless, our eyes shielded by dark sunglasses. One by one, we held up a paper showing a score of one or two, indicating that he had lost the championship.

"Ah," Bill muttered in disgust before walking away.

Then, the other man approached; he looked fresh, was barely sweating, and was breathing normally. We each held up a sign showing ten—a perfect score. The crowd cheered and applauded, but we remained expressionless.

"Hey, thanks a lot, guys," Bill muttered. We all just stared at him. "I get no respect."

The director yelled, "Cut," and we all laughed.

"Good job, everyone," Bill declared. "Okay, I want to joust with my son for this next scene."

"What? Come on, Dad, I can't ride a horse!"

"No, not on horses; see that wooden bridge over there? It's a spot for two people to use long poles to battle. The bridge is narrow, has no rails, and is built over a mud puddle. The winner is the one who knocks the other off the bridge into the mud."

"Okay, let me get this straight: You want me to take a stick and knock you into the mud? Is this for real? I mean, what if I hurt you?"

"Boy, you can't touch me. I will be victorious, and you will be muddy."

"You're on, old man."

The two of them marched over to the bridge,

followed by the crowd, as the film crew continued filming. Bill stripped off his armor and approached from one side of the bridge while Ben came from the other. They met in the middle, using the poles to balance themselves on the narrow bridge, and began the smack talk.

"Give up now, boy; you're no match for my strength. I can just push you off using my weight because you're a skinny kid."

"Listen, fatso, I may be skinny, but I'm quick, agile, and I'm gonna make you eat a mud pie."

Father and son lunged at each other, clashing their poles together sideways. Each time they lunged, the other shifted and swayed, trying to keep their balance and jab with their pole against their opponent. Several times, Bill nearly had Ben down. Each time, he exclaimed "Aha!" but Ben sprang back up without falling off the bridge.

The crowd cheered, some for Ben and some for Bill. Then suddenly, Ben bent down and swung his pole at the back of Bill's knees. This caused Bill's knees to buckle involuntarily, making him lose his balance and fall off the bridge into the mud.

Bill stood up in the mud and sighed. The crowd went wild, applauding and cheering for the winner, Ben. Ben held his pole high and marched off the bridge to help his dad get out of the mud.

Just as Ben was about to pull him out, Bill yanked Ben into the mud face first. The crowd erupted once more, laughing and clapping. The two mud wrestlers were now laughing so hard that they couldn't stand. Every time they tried to get out of the mud, they slipped and fell back in. Soon, they were completely covered. I simply shook my head.

"Hey, Cara, come here and help me out," Ben yelled, extending his mud-drenched hand.

"Not for any amount of money, Benjamin Bates!"

Soon, the crew dug both Bates out of the mud and hosed them down. They were still quite damp, but the day was warm, and they would dry off before long.

Afterward, Bill and the crew went to film interviews with some of the castle staff, leaving Ben and me to wander on our own. Soon, we were surrounded by a roaming minstrel band, drawing us into dancing with them. What a delight to bounce, sway, and laugh! They taught us some dance moves, gathering a crowd as we danced in costume to the music. When the music stopped, we received a round of applause. So, Ben and I bowed to the audience before running off, giggling.

We walked hand in hand, sneaking kisses here and there until it was time to pack up the van and head to the Globe Theatre. We returned our costumes and jumped back into the van. Bill said, "Punch it," and we took off.

When we arrived, the crew got busy setting up the cameras, lights, and other equipment at the theater.

Nana found a seat to rest in and said, "Let me know when y'all are ready to leave." She took a book out of her backpack and began to read.

Ben, Liam, and I wandered around as I read aloud from a brochure. "According to this brochure I picked up at the hotel, this theater is a replica of the original built in the 1500s by Richard Burbage. The original burned down due to a cannon mishap that occurred during the play Henry VIII."

"Wait a minute. They fired a cannon inside the building?" Ben asked.

"Yeah, I guess so."

"No wonder it burned down."

"It was rebuilt but was torn down again by the Puritans some years later. William Shakespeare bought shares in the theater and benefited financially as his popularity grew. Oh, this is interesting; they would hang colored flags outside to let people know what kind of performance was scheduled. A red flag for a history play, white for a comedy, and black for a tragedy."

"Cara, what does that sign above the door say?" Liam asked, pointing to the crest above the main entrance.

"I'm not sure, Liam. It's written in Latin."

"It says, *Totus mundus agit histrionem*—Latin for 'The whole world is a playhouse,'" Ben said.

"Wow, you can read Latin?" I asked him.

He laughed. "Not really; I think my dad told me about the Shakespearean motto over this door."

"I'm going to look around," Liam declared as he walked off.

"Do you think we should stop him?" I asked Ben.

"Nah, he can't go far. Let him explore."

Ben and I sat and chatted, scrolled through Twitter feeds and YouTube videos, and enjoyed each other's company. Finally, the crew was ready to film some clips, so they called us over.

"So, where's my little buddy?" Mr. Bates asked. "The crew thinks he'll be a great way to attract a younger audience if I interact with him."

"I'm not sure. Hold on. Liam!" I called out. No answer. "Liam!"

Nothing but crickets.

I sighed. "Sorry, it seems he's off on another misadventure. I should probably go find him." As I marched away, seething, Ben followed.

"I'll help look for him. I'll be right back, Dad," he yelled over his shoulder.

I stomped behind the stage, ready to grab my brother by the hair. I was so tired of having to search for him. He was old enough to know better than to wander off!

"Hey, wait up," pleaded Ben. "Why are you running?"

"Liam talks nonstop about wanting to go on an adventure with Bill Bates, and then he wanders off just when it's time to leave! I'm so tired of chasing after him! This is another reason I wish my dad were around. Let him take a turn chasing after the brat. I just want to have some fun for once without worrying about Liam," I snapped.

Ben held up his hands. "Sorry, calm down. Everything's going to be okay."

"No, it's not. Dad will spend two weeks with us and then take off again for God knows how long. The military will send him here and there, and he'll miss Liam's whole childhood." Tears began to slip from the corners of my eyes, and I quickly brushed them away.

Ben wrapped his arms around me. "I'm sorry. But it seems to me that you need to tell your dad how you feel."

I sighed. "You're probably right, but I don't want him to worry. He has an important job to do. How do I share my concerns when he already has so much on his plate?"

Ben shrugged. "I don't know. I have trouble talking to my dad, too."

He looked thoughtful for a moment and then snapped his fingers. "I've got it! How about we swap dads for a day? I'll talk to your dad about how you're feeling, and you can talk to my dad about how I'm feeling."

I rolled my eyes. "Sure, that'll work."

"You got any better ideas?"

"No. Let's figure this out later; right now, we gotta find my ridiculously curious, wandering little brother."

"Liam!" I called.

"Liam!" Ben called.

"Look, Ben, what's that over there? Let's check it out."

Ben and I hurried to the area where we found boxes of costumes and props scattered about. Behind all the clutter was a hidden door. It was barely cracked open—just enough space for a small boy to wiggle through.

"Leave it to that boy to find a hidden door." I pulled out my phone, activated the flashlight app, and shone it into the space behind the door. "Looks like a passageway. He must have gone down here. Come on, we'd better follow."

We moved more boxes and then pushed the door open wide enough for us to squeeze through. Ben and I walked down the dirt-floored passageway, brushing aside cobwebs as we went. It was dirty and dark, with a damp smell in the air. I coughed and brushed the dust off my clothes as we moved. It was clear that no one had been down here for years.

I called for Liam and heard him reply, "I'm down here."

As we turned a corner, Liam stood before another door. It looked ancient, straight out of a medieval castle. Made of wood, it was much larger than a normal door, with rusty hinges and a rusty doorknob.

"I've tried, but I can't get this door open," Liam said.

"Liam, we shouldn't be down here. We don't have permission," I scolded

"But Cara, don't you wanna see what's on the other side of this door?"

I had to admit, I was curious about what lay behind that door. "What do you think, Ben?"

"Heck, yeah! I'm with Liam; let's crack this sucker open."

Liam burst into a smile. Ben examined the doorknob and the keyhole. It was a large keyhole, likely meant for an old skeleton key. Ben looked around, feeling along the dirt floor until he found a rusty old nail.

"Ah ha," he muttered. He plunged the nail into the keyhole, jiggled it around, and, after a few minutes, heard a click. He grinned as he turned the doorknob and gently pulled the door open. "And that's how it's done!"

Liam leaped toward the door, but I yanked him back. "Hold on, mister. Remember *Raiders of the Lost Ark*? Let's go slow and check for traps, holes, or creepy crawly bugs."

He nodded in agreement.

"I'll go first," Ben offered. He slowly opened the door fully, and it creaked loudly, sounding like a door in a haunted house. It made me shiver. He shone his phone's flashlight inside, revealing a long, narrow corridor with a dirt floor that led down into the darkness.

"Well, Liam, it seems this is going to be your greatest misadventure ever," I said.

A voice behind us chimed in, "I agree!"

We all jumped, and I let out a shriek. My heart raced; someone had crept up behind us. We turned quickly to see who was there.

Chapter 7:
My Captain, Oh Captain

Aboard the USS Enterprise, Captain O'Connor contemplated his coming leave time.

I stared blankly at the Bible page, not reading, just contemplating. Worries about my kids and mother disrupted my usual morning routine of reading the Bible and enjoying coffee. They were stuck in England due to the dust storm in Cairo.

I glanced at my packed duffle bag. I was supposed to join them in Cairo today, but now it has been postponed. I've been away too long and didn't want any delays in reuniting with them. My ship was docked in Gibraltar, Spain, only a few hours away by helicopter.

I sighed, closed the book, and began to pray. "Lord, help me get to them without delay. Protect them while they are in a foreign land."

Just as I finished, there was a knock at the door.

"Enter."

My chief petty officer, Max Savage, opened the door and stepped inside, closing it behind him. "Good morning, Captain. I hate to interrupt, but we have a situation that I need to bring to your attention immediately."

"What is it?"

"I'm bringing in Seaman Johnson to explain what's happening." Max reached over and opened the door once more, and Seaman Randy Johnson stepped inside.

Randy stood at attention, waiting for one of us senior officers to give him permission to speak.

"Captain Seaman Johnson operates the sonar on the ship and has detected an unauthorized transmission originating from within the vessel, directed toward an area known for ISIS activity. Please repeat what you told me to the captain."

"Yes, sir. Captain, this began last night when we took on temporary duty foreign exchange officers. My duty shift starts at 2100 hours. Around 0200 hours, I was monitoring the sonar for activity when I noticed some unusual sounds.

"Initially, I thought it was an equipment issue and attempted to adjust for the static, but I soon noticed it had a distinct pattern. I speculated that it might be Morse code, so I recorded the messages.

Once decoded, the message didn't make any sense to me, so I decided to try a different approach. I input the message into an interpretation program and translated it into English. The messages are in Arabic and were sent to a location here in Spain known to be associated with ISIS."

My heart raced as I leaned forward on my elbows. My blood pressure spiked and pounded in my ears. I was furious. Someone was communicating with the enemy on my ship! My face tightened as I contemplated this information. "Seaman, what did the messages say?"

"Sir, they were coordinates: 31° 12' 20.7108" N latitude and 29° 55' 28.2936" E longitude. These coordinates point to our next port of call, Alexandria."

I turned to the chief. "What do you think, Max?"

"It sounds like they're planning a surprise for us when we arrive in Alexandria."

"Sounds like it to me, too. Seaman, can you trace where those communications are coming from inside the ship?"

"Yes, sir, I've already done that. They're coming from the guest quarters on deck four, starboard side."

"Chief, grab a couple of NCIS officers and meet Seaman Johnson and me at those quarters."

"Aye, Captain," both men replied.

I strapped on my holster and service weapon, grabbed my cap, and stepped out the door. Seaman

Johnson led the way through the depths of the ship toward the guest quarters. Navy personnel parted in the crowded hallways to make way for us and stood at attention as I walked by. They looked curious and concerned to see me following Seaman Johnson while carrying my pistol. Given my stern expression, no one dared ask what was happening.

We arrived at the quarters of one of the British naval officers, shortly followed by the chief and two NCIS officers. A Middle Eastern-looking man dressed in a British naval uniform answered my knock. His eyes widened when he saw me in the doorway.

"Captain? I, uh, wasn't expecting you, I, uh," he stuttered.

"Name, Lieutenant!" I barked.

The man jumped to attention. "Yes, sir. Lieutenant Amin Ackbar, sir."

I stepped aside and pointed to the NCIS officers. One of the officers interjected, saying to Amin, "You are under arrest pending an investigation for espionage." He was quickly handcuffed and taken away.

"Search his rack, tear the place apart, and find that communication device," I shouted. Seaman Johnson, the other NCIS officer, and the chief sprang into action as curious onlookers peeked in from the hallway. I stepped out of the cabin and bellowed, "Back to work!" People scattered like frightened rats.

"Chief," I said.

"Yes, sir?"

"I'm heading topside. Let me know what you find."

"Aye, Captain."

Back in the corridor, I trudged toward the bridge with a heavy heart, thinking, *Lord, didn't I just pray for no delays in getting to my kids? This feels like a significant delay. But I will have to trust you.*

"Captain on the bridge," announced Yeoman Higgins.

I was so lost in thought that I hadn't even realized I'd reached the bridge. I snapped out of worry mode and focused all my attention on my crew and my work for the day. "Good morning, everyone."

There were "Good morning, Captain" responses from all around me.

As I sat down in my chair overlooking the bridge, Yeoman Higgins handed me a report.

"Your morning report, Captain," she remarked, tilting her head to the side as she stared into my face. "Is something wrong, Captain? You look more stressed than usual this morning."

I sighed. *This girl is really good at her job. She must have a sixth sense; she always knows when I'm trying to hide something.* "I'm fine, Yeoman," I muttered, aware that wouldn't satisfy her.

"Captain," she reminded me, "part of my job is

to look after your needs. If you won't confide in me about what's troubling you, then at least let me get you some coffee or something to eat."

I nodded absently as I poured over the report. "Okay, a cup of coffee would be great, thanks."

I was too anxious to sit for long. After reviewing the morning report from the night shift and finding nothing unusual, I walked around the bridge, gathering reports on the weather, coordinates, and other operational conditions. When Yeoman Higgins returned, I sat and sipped my coffee, drumming my fingers on the side table impatiently as I waited for the chief to arrive and update me on our spy.

The door to the bridge opened, and the chief walked in. "My ready room, Chief." I indicated the door behind me with a nod of my head, and the chief and I went into a closed session.

"Well, what did you find?"

"We found a VHF DSC radio, sir. We also contacted his superiors in England, and they demanded that we hand him and the evidence over to them for trial as soon as possible. We can have a helicopter ready in fifteen minutes, sir. After that, he will be the Brits' problem, not ours."

"What about his accomplices?"

"The British detectives assure me they can obtain the terrorist's coordinates from the radio and apprehend them before the ship reaches Egypt.

They promised to keep us updated on every aspect of their investigation. I believe the ship is safe enough for you to be with your family. Sir, I recommend you accompany our NCIS officer and the spy to England. You can catch up with your family before they leave for Egypt."

I contemplated that remark for a minute. It was hard to think about leaving when there was any chance something could happen to the ship. But I had prayed for no delays in getting to my kids, and this was an answer to that prayer.

I grinned at Max, slapped him on the back, and said, "The bridge is yours, Chief." I practically skipped down the corridor to my quarters to grab my bags. I didn't even stop to call my mom and let her know. It would be a totally wonderful surprise when I showed up at their hotel tonight. I couldn't wait.

True to the chief's word, I was flying away in our navy helicopter within fifteen minutes. As I strapped myself in, I noticed Lieutenant Akbar was also there, handcuffed between two stern, fully armed marines, and one NCIS officer was beside me. They saluted, except Akbar, who glared at me.

I nodded to the others. "Gentlemen."

"You don't have enough evidence to convict me, Captain," Amin said. "It will go better for you and your family if you let me go when we get to England."

I narrowed my eyes at him. "Are you threatening me?"

One of the marines turned toward Amin, raised his fist, and jerked his arm. "Shut up, or you'll get more than you bargained for."

"At ease, Marine," I said.

"Captain," Akbar continued. "We know where your mother and children are right now. All I'm saying is for you to think about their safety before you press charges." He gave an evil grin.

I stared at him for a few seconds, holding back the urge to slam my fist into his ugly face, then said to the marine, "Gag him." For the rest of the trip, there was silence.

Once we arrived at Heathrow, the gag was removed from the prisoner. The NCIS officer and the marines marched Armin off, while I headed to catch the bus to my families hotel. As he was led away, he turned to me and said, "We will meet again, my captain, oh Captain."

Again, I thought he was lucky that I hadn't brought my service weapon.

Chapter 8:
Escaped

Amin walked through Heathrow Airport handcuffed, with two armed marines on either side of him and the US Navy NCIS officer leading the way. *At least they took the gag off my mouth*, he thought. He'd made one call to shore before he left on the helicopter. He said he was calling his lawyer, but he wasn't. He had spoken to an associate in Spain, warning them to move their headquarters. He had spoken in Farsi, so none of the clueless navy personnel understood his conversation.

People stared, pointed, and whispered as the group passed, but Amin ignored them. He noticed several men seated in chairs along the way and smiled. A few of these men began to follow his small group discreetly.

Halfway through the airport, two officers from Scotland Yard approached them and took Amin into custody. The NCIS officer and the marines returned to their waiting helicopter and flew back to the ship.

Once they were out of sight, Amin said, "Come on, gents, I need to use the loo." Both men frowned and rolled their eyes.

One of them nodded to the right. "Up on the right then," he said, "and make it quick." One detective waited outside the restroom while the other accompanied Amin inside. He unlocked Amin's handcuffs and leaned back against the wall to wait. Amin stepped into a stall, shut the door, and locked it. One of the men following the group slipped into the stall next to Amin, unnoticed, as the detective was on his phone, texting.

A few minutes later, two more of the men who'd followed the group came into the room and stood at the sink washing their hands. One splashed water on the other, which started a heated argument and a shoving match. The detective waiting beside Amin's door jumped in to break up the fuss before there was a fist fight.

Several people exited quickly to avoid getting involved with the problem, including a man in a red hoodie, who had it pulled up over his head. He walked rapidly and did not look back. The second detective stood in the hallway, scrolling through his phone, oblivious to the chaos around him and indifferent to those leaving the restroom.

Things returned to normal, and the two men left. After about fifteen minutes, the detective knocked on

Amin's stall door. "Hey now, mate, are you done yet?"

There was no answer. The detective waited a moment and tried again, but still no response. He peeked under the stall door and didn't see any feet.

"Bugger!" he yelled toward the door. "Oy, Mike, get in here and bring the janitor."

Mike rushed in along with the janitor. "Is something wrong, gents?" the janitor asked.

"Do you have a key to open this loo?"

"Aye," the janitor said, pulling a key from his pocket and opening the door. Amin was gone, and a duffle bag with his navy uniform was on the floor.

Both detectives cursed and ran out into the hallway. "You go right, and I'll go left," yelled Mike. They split and raced through the hallway, but there was no sign of Amin.

"Call security," Mike said to the janitor. "Let them know we're on our way to their office to review the video feed. Our prisoner has escaped, and he's disguised himself."

The janitor nodded and grabbed his radio to contact security while the two detectives raced off toward the security office.

Meanwhile, Amin rounded a corner out of sight of the cameras, slipped off his red hoodie, and tossed it into a nearby trash bin. One of the men following him dropped a duffle bag next to him and stood watch as Amin changed his shirt, added a new jacket, and put on a wool hat. Then, the two of them stood and walked toward the front door.

They remained silent, trying to be as inconspicuous as possible. As they rode the escalator down the stairs, men in security uniforms began to rush in all directions. The two men could see the front door directly across from the escalator. They kept going. They stepped outside and hailed a taxi just as the security personnel gathered by the front door, blocking the exit for everyone behind them.

As the taxi sped away toward their safe house, Amin and his companion glanced back to see if they were being followed. No one was behind them. They smiled at each other, clasped hands in a brotherly handshake, and let out a loud sigh. They began a conversation in Farsi, assuming the driver would not understand them.

"Thank you, my friend," Amin said.

"That was close," replied his companion. "What will you do now since our plans to blow up the naval vessel are foiled?"

"Ah, but it is not over yet," replied Amin with an evil laugh. "I have a new plan. I heard the captain telling the first officer his itinerary. He will be with his family in Egypt for the next two weeks. He left his ship without a weapon, nor does he have his personnel surrounding him to protect him. We will kidnap his family and hold them for ransom, threatening to kill them until he does everything we demand."

"What will you demand? Surely, he will not blow up his ship?"

"No, but he will send rockets to Tel Aviv or Jerusalem if he wants his family back safe." That saying made Amin's companion smile and nod his head. "For tonight, we will lay low and plan our strategy to capture the captain's family."

Chapter 9:
Stowaway

Bill Bates and his crew stood behind us with their arms crossed, except for the cameraman, John, who was filming.

"Well?" Bill asked, glancing at his son.

Ben let out a loud breath. "Dad, you spooked us. We found Liam, and he discovered this hidden passage. We're going in. Do you want to come?"

"You better believe it!" Bill said with a smile. "Finally, I get to go on an adventure with my son!" He clapped Ben on the back.

"And me, don't forget me!" Liam chimed in.

"How could I forget you, little buddy? You found our next big mystery to solve."

Liam smiled. "Did you hear that, Cara? I found Bill Bates's next big adventure."

"I heard. Congratulations."

Turning to his crew, Bill said, "Okay, Mike, go let our host know about this door. We'll wait a few minutes for him to catch up and join us through the secret passage. Ben, open John's backpack and grab some flashlights."

John stopped filming and took off his backpack. Ben reached inside and pulled out three flashlights and a headlamp. Bill put on the headlamp as Ben handed out the other lights. Soon, the corridor was bathed in a soft, shadowy glow.

"Okay, guys, start filming on my mark. Three, two, one, mark," said the director, pointing at Bill. The cameras blinked red, and more lights turned on.

Bill looked into the camera and said, "We are at the Shakespeare Globe Theatre in London, where my son, Ben, our little buddy Liam, and his sister, Cara, have discovered a hidden passage. We're about to enter and hope to uncover where this corridor leads and what treasures may be hidden here."

Marcus, our host for the day, entered the room and peered into the passageway as the crew continued filming. "This is remarkable! I don't think this is on any of our maps or drawings. It's a real secret passage. I believe this must have been constructed beneath the original Globe Theatre. What a historical find! Our archaeologists will be thrilled."

"Shall we continue to explore this passage, Marcus?" Bill asked.

"Yes, absolutely, please go ahead, Bill!"

Bill continued to narrate as he and the film crew led the way. The passage descended about ten feet, leveled off, and stretched straight ahead. "We are passing through a corridor of mud brick walls interspersed with hand-hewn wooden beams. Wooden beams are also on the ceiling above us, with a dirt floor beneath. We are moving further underground. It looks like there's an opening up ahead. Yes, it appears to be a small room at the end."

Before long, we all squeezed into the room filled with wooden crates, old barrel trunks, and shelves lined with bags, jars, and other items.

"Look at this! This is unbelievable! A hidden room beneath the Globe Theatre. No one has seen this for hundreds of years," Bill exclaimed.

"What is this place?" I asked.

"I think it's a treasure room; maybe it belonged to pirates!" Liam exclaimed.

"No, I believe it's a prop and costume area," Bill replied. "Look, there's a wooden goblet on this shelf, a wooden sword leaned against the wall, a costume folded next to the goblet, and this rolled-up parchment beside it. I wouldn't dare touch it; it's so old it might fall apart in my hands."

"Please, let's refrain from touching any parchments without gloves," Marcus said. "Everything in this room needs to be properly cataloged and recorded for posterity, after which it will be housed in a museum where it can be cared for or displayed permanently."

Liam shouted excitedly, jumping up and down, "I found a gold coin!" He rushed over to show it to Bill.

"Oh my word!" Mr. Bates exclaimed as he examined Liam's coin. "It is indeed a gold coin. It appears to be from the time of Shakespeare. What do you think, Marcus?"

Marcus inspected the coin. "Yes, it's from the era of Queen Elizabeth the First. See, here is her image. I would expect this to go to the British Museum right away."

"Wait a minute! I found it! Finder's keepers, losers weepers—right, Mr. Bates? I found it, so I get to keep it."

Bill glanced at Liam and then at the camera, sighing. He leaned closer to the camera and whispered, "This is why we don't bring little kids on our expeditions."

Then Bill turned to Liam, kneeled to meet his gaze, and gently explained that anything they discover on an expedition belongs to the country where it's found. Their contract states they can't remove items from the country for personal use.

"Sorry, buddy, but you must give up the coin."

Liam looked sad but agreed. "Okay. If you promise not to keep anything, I can, too."

"Let's shake on that," Bill said, extending his

hand to Liam. Liam took Bill's hand and shook it vigorously, grinning widely.

We carefully examined the items in the room for hours, filming the entire time. We uncovered one treasure after another, becoming completely absorbed in the moment as Bill continued to film and narrate each discovery.

After a while, the crew was tired, and Bill called it a day. We all marched back the way we had come until we reached the large medieval door, which was closed and locked.

"Oh, oh, looks like the door is locked," one of the crew members said. Several guys pushed against it with their shoulders, but it wouldn't budge.

"Now what?" someone asked.

"I'll call Nana; maybe she can open it from the outside," I suggested.

I had no service. "Does anyone have cell service?"

Everyone checked their phones, trying to dial out. Nothing.

"There must be some interference underground," Marcus remarked.

Liam pounded on the door. "Hey, Nana, come open the door!" No answer.

Bill sighed. "Okay, everyone, let's give it a few minutes and see if Nana comes to rescue us." We all sat on the cold ground and waited.

Suddenly, Nana swung the door open and marched into the room. She stood with her hands on her hips and said, "Listen, everyone. It's late, it's getting dark, and it's dinner time. You'll have to come back tomorrow to finish your exploring."

We all laughed.

Soon, we were on our way to the pub for one last meal together before we headed off to Egypt and our separate ways in the morning. Part of me hoped we could have one more day together, or at least that I could get some additional time alone with Ben. I sighed. Wishful thinking, Cara, wishful thinking.

At dinner, Ben and I managed to sit next to each other. As the rest of the group discussed the hidden treasures, Ben whispered, "This may be our last night together."

I nodded. "I know. I'm a bit sad, Ben; I've really enjoyed being with you. "

He reached under the table and took my hand. He was quiet for a moment, then leaned over and whispered, "I'm sad too. Do you want to sneak out again and have one more fun night with me? We can go to that event Mr. Hennison told us about."

I nodded. "Same time?"

He nodded.

"Okay, I'll meet you downstairs around eleven."

Once we returned to the hotel, I grabbed my journal.

114

Once Nana and Liam fell asleep, I sneaked downstairs to meet Ben.

"I have a surprise; we're going to a silent dance party," Ben said.

"What's that?"

"All the partygoers wear headsets, and a DJ streams music into them, so we can hear it and dance, but it doesn't fill the air. It's going to be off the fly!"

The party was within walking distance. When we entered, they handed us headsets. We put them on, and it was incredible. We danced, we laughed, and when we took the headsets off, the only sound was the stomping of feet. We stayed until one o'clock and then headed home.

We held hands all the way to my door, where Ben kissed me good night. I lingered in the hallway for a few more minutes, thinking of Ben, then slowly opened the door. I tiptoed in, trying not to make a noise, when suddenly, the lights turned on. I froze. Standing in the middle of the room with their arms crossed were Nana and Dad, glaring at me.

Well, this misadventure just went to caca!

"Um, hi, Dad. What are you doing here?"

He just stood there, glaring at me. I swear, steam and fire were coming out of his nostrils.

"Your father wanted to surprise you and Liam by meeting us in London. Imagine my concern when I woke up and you weren't here. I nearly had a heart attack. Obviously, you went somewhere with Ben. Where did you go?" demanded Nana.

Crap, I was so excited to meet Ben that I forgot to leave a note. "We, um, went to a club and danced a little, that's all. We didn't stay very long. Nothing happened. We're just friends."

"We texted you; we called you, and you didn't respond," said Dad.

"We had headsets on. It was a silent dance party, so I didn't hear the phone. Sorry."

"Sorry! Is that all you have to say? I was ready to call the police. I didn't know if you were hurt in a traffic accident, mugged, kidnapped, or what was going on. "Did you drink at this club?" Dad asked.

Don't lie, Cara! "No, not this time."

"What do you mean, not this time? Have you done this before? Have you gone out drinking after curfew with this boy before tonight?"

Now you've done it! Don't lie; just get it over with.

"Um, yeah, but I had one sip of a local beer, and it tasted so awful that I didn't have any more. I swear, I thought it was root beer."

Dad pointed his finger and started yelling at me, but Liam snored, snorted, and turned over in his sleep, so Dad lowered his voice to an angry whisper. "I am very disappointed in you, young lady. I expected more from you than this kind of behavior."

That's when I lost it.

"What, Dad? What were you expecting? Since the day Mom died, I've done everything expected of me. I do my chores, keep my grades up, and chase after Liam on his crazy adventures every day!"

My voice started to rise. All the stress from the past few months, the worry about losing my last parent in a war zone, and all the fun things I'd put off with my friends to help take care of my kid brother—it all came rushing back to me.

"My friends are all going on dates, going to the prom, being normal teenagers, but not me. I have to be the mom. Nana loves us and takes good care of us, but it's too much for her to do all alone. She never complains, but I can see how exhausted she is every night. So, where were you, Dad? Why can't you be home with us?"

Tears streamed down my face.

"It's been this way since Mom died! You're never there when we get home from school. You miss all our school ceremonies and soccer games. This was my first real date with a boy I really liked. We didn't do anything wrong," I sobbed.

"We never even talk about her. We all walk around with grief and pain. Some days, I don't even want to get out of bed. Worst of all, I can't remember her voice!" I cried. After all these years of missing my mom and trying to live without her, I suddenly felt overwhelmed.

There was silence for a few minutes, and no one spoke. Nana wiped the tears from her eyes. My dad hung his head. I sobbed quietly, realizing I had hurt him with my words.

"I'm sorry, Dad. I love you." He reached over and hugged me tight. I sobbed into his shirt.

"Shh, it's okay. I'm sorry, too. I love you so much. I know it's been hard on you since Mom died. You have done a great job helping Nana. I'm so proud of you and the responsible woman you have become. But you're still my baby girl, and if I ever meet that boy, I may have to shoot him."

I laughed. Liam opened his eyes and sat up. "What's going on?" he asked sleepily. Then he saw Dad. "Dad!" he yelled, jumping from the bed into Dad's arms. Dad caught him just in time.

"Whoa, buddy, you almost knocked me over. Man, you've grown so much!"

I turned away and found some tissue to dry my

eyes; I didn't want Liam to worry. When I turned around, I forced a smile onto my face, but my heart still ached.

"Dad, we're going on an adventure with Bill Bates! Do you want to come with us? We're going to find tombs and bones and treasure…" and he was off talking nonstop.

It would be another hour before everyone settled down to sleep. Liam snuggled in one bed with Dad while Nana and I cuddled up in the other. Even with Nana's snoring, I slept soundly because I knew my whole family was together.

The next day, we packed up and met the Bates team at the airport to leave for Cairo, Egypt. From there, we would go our separate ways. When we arrived at our departing gate, Ben and his dad approached us. I introduced them to my dad.

My dad crossed his arms and glared at Ben. "So, this is the boy who took you to a club to dance and drink?" My eyes widened, and I gulped.

Mr. Bates looked astonished. "He did what?"

He turned and stood beside my dad, crossed his arms, and glared at Ben. They looked like two angry gorillas.

OMG, Ben is a dead man!

Ben's eyes widened as he glanced from his dad to mine and back again. "I, um, well, I sorta, kinda…" he sputtered.

He turned to me, and I mouthed the word *Sorry*.

He looked at the dads and mumbled, "Yes, sir," then quickly added, "But nothing happened. Really. I'm sorry, sir."

My dad glanced at his dad and said, "I don't think he's truly sorry."

His dad turned to my dad and replied, "I agree. What do you think we should do about him?"

My dad said, "Well, I seriously considered shooting him, but I couldn't bring my service weapon on the plane."

His dad nodded. "Yep, and that would have been very messy, with blood all over the place. We could tie him to the outside of the airplane and make him ride on the wing."

My dad nodded. "True, but that might make it harder for the pilot to maintain control. The plane would be unbalanced. We could shave his head and remove all the lovely hair. Girls his age wouldn't want to date a bald boy."

"Well, if we're going to shave his head, we might as well enroll him in the military. What branch are you in?"

"I'm in the navy. I'm the captain of my vessel, so if you put him in the navy, I can assign him to my ship. Now, wouldn't that be something?"

They both turned and gave Ben an evil grin.

"No, come on, Dad, this isn't funny. I can't go into the navy!"

"So, is there a recruiting office in Boston?"

"Sure, give me your phone number, and I'll text it to you."

The two men pulled out their phones. I could see Ben starting to sweat. Just then, the announcement came: *Now boarding flight 623 to Cairo at gate thirty-six. Business class may now board.*

"We have to board now, so we'll finish this when we land," said Mr. Bates as the men put away their phones.

We began to board. "Are you guys in business-class seats?' my dad asked.

"Yeah, Nana's butt was hurting, so we got bigger seats," yelled Liam as people turned to stare.

"Shh, Liam, not so loud," Nana whispered.

"Well, that leaves me out. I have a cheap seat. I'll see you guys when we get to Egypt."

"No, listen, I have three seats. I'll sit with my son, and you can have the extra seat to be near your kids."

"No, I couldn't ask you to do that."

"It's not a problem. Let's call it a thank you for your service. Besides, my son and I need to talk."

Ben gulped and turned a bit pale.

So, we boarded the plane. Liam sat with Dad;

Nana and I sat together in front of them; and Ben, with his dad, sat toward the back of the business class.

This trip wasn't as long as the one to London. Every time I turned to check on Ben, he and his dad were deep in discussion. Liam didn't stop talking, and Dad loved it; he missed his little boy and wanted to hear all about his misadventures.

Finally, we landed in Cairo, where we gathered outside the airport's front door to bid our final goodbyes to the Bates group. The sun was hot, and the air was dry. Some men stood around, filling the air with cigarette smoke. Some stood by cabs, holding open doors and yelling for people to hop in. Others sat on the low wall and glared at the foreigners pouring out of the airport, pointing toward the pyramids in amazement.

I approached Ben. "I just wanted to thank you for last night. I'm sorry about my dad. I have your number, so maybe we could catch up on WhatsApp, or you can text me once in a while to let me know how you're doing."

Ben smiled. "I'd like that. Your dad is a scary dude, but sitting together on the plane gave my dad and me a chance to clear the air. I told him I wanted to study marine biology. I also confessed that I felt neglected when he's always off on these adventures. He understood, and we scheduled the next time we would be together during fall break into our phones. He promised not to bring the crew."

"That's wonderful! I'm so happy for you."

I looked around, and everyone watched us, waiting for us to wrap up. "Well, take care, Ben."

He leaned in as if he wanted to kiss me, but when he saw my dad frowning at him with tightly crossed arms, he awkwardly extended his hand, grabbed mine, and shook it up and down. My whole upper body was moving. "Well, bye now, take care... um, later."

As Dad selected a cab, Liam ran over to where the Bates crew was loading a large truck with equipment. "Mr. Bates, am I going with you today? Are you going to the pyramids? Can my family come too?"

Mr. Bates sighed and squatted down to Liam's eye level. "Liam, you are an awesome kid. I love your zest for life and your thirst for adventure, but I think you need to spend time with your family right now, okay?"

Liam looked down and sighed, "Yeah, okay."

Mr. Bates patted him on the back, and Liam slowly walked back to our group. Dad was negotiating a fare with the cab driver for our ride to the hotel while Nana and I admired the pyramids we could see in the distance.

"I had no idea they were that big!" said Nana.

I had my phone out, snapping pictures. "I'm so excited. I can't wait to get up closer."

"Okay, everyone. I got the cab driver to agree to a reasonable price, so hop in, and let's get going. Cara, where's Liam?" Dad asked.

"He went over to talk to the Bateses, but then he came back."

I looked around. "Liam? Liam, where are you? Stop fooling around and get over here." I didn't see him anywhere.

"I'll check if he's in the bathroom," said Dad.

"I'll ask the Bates group if they've seen him. Nana, you wait here and keep our cab driver from leaving."

I walked toward the Bates team's truck, but it pulled away just as I started to approach it. As it passed, I waved goodbye to Ben and his dad. I stared after them, and that's when I saw it—the tarp in the back moved, and up popped a small head. It was Liam! He smiled at me, waved goodbye, then popped his head back into the truck.

OMG! Liam did it. He stowed away on a great adventure with Bill Bates. Doggone that kid! Why did I ever show him that TV series?

"Dad," I yelled. "We have a problem."

Dad came running over. "Did you find him?"

I pointed to the Bateses' truck pulling away. "He's off on another misadventure. He's a stowaway on the Bateses' caravan."

"He's where?"

"On the truck, Dad!"

Dad looked at the truck and swore under his breath.

"Language! You are not on your ship, Captain!" Nana exclaimed.

"Sorry."

"Dad, I'll text Ben and tell him to turn around," I said, pulling out my phone.

While I typed, Dad had a heated conversation with the cab driver, who complained about losing money waiting for us.

"Dad, Ben must have his phone off; he's not answering."

Dad took his phone out of his pocket. "Bill gave me his number; let me try calling them. It's ringing, but there's no answer. They probably can't hear the phone because of the loud truck noises. I'm leaving a message.

"Hello, Bill, it's Vic. Liam is hiding in your truck. We couldn't reach you, so we're heading to Dahshur. I'm sorry, but we'll be there as soon as we can. Please let us know exactly where you are so we can meet you and return my wayward child. Thanks."

He hung up and put his phone in his pocket.

In the meantime, the cab driver found another fare, left our stuff on the sidewalk, and drove away. Dad took a while but finally found a truck to take us to Dahshur. It was a rusty, beat-up mess, but it had enough room for everyone to sit. The inside was filthy, with no air conditioning and a smell of diesel fuel, but at least it was moving.

As we got ready to leave, the Bates team called us back. "Yes, do you have my boy?" Dad asked. "Oh, thank God. Yes, we're on our way. The Marriott? Okay. Could you put the front desk on the phone? I'm going to need a room. It's getting late, and we're exhausted. Looks like we'll spend the night. Dinner? Yes, that would be great. Thanks. Okay, bye."

Dad booked a room and then hung up the phone. He was quiet for a minute. I held my breath as Dad sighed and then spoke. "We're going to stay the night at the Marriott hotel, have dinner with the Bates team, and continue to Giza in the morning."

My heart leaped—another night to be close to Ben. I stared into space, smiling and thinking about him, when a face suddenly came into view. My smile faded as I recognized my dad, who was frowning at me.

"And there will be no sneaking out to be with your boyfriend! Understand?!" I nodded. *Man, I would hate to be a sailor on his ship. He's scary.*

As the family drove away, a small black car with two men followed.

The passenger said to the driver, "Follow them.' He pulled out his phone and quickly dialed. "Amin, it is Banha. I thought these people were going to Giza, but they're heading the opposite way?"

"What! Follow them. Don't let them get away. Where are they headed?"

"It looks like they're following the American explorer toward Dahshur. I don't know why, but this will make it easier for us to catch them. There are fewer crowds."

"That's good. Yes, catch them and bring them to me immediately. I look forward to seeing the fear on my captain's face when I tie up his lovely daughter and his precious son and hold a gun to their heads."

"We'll follow them, but keep our distance. We don't want to give away our presence. We must catch them unaware when they exit the truck at their destination.

"Agreed. Go with Allah."

Banha and the driver continued to follow the O'Connors' truck for miles, discussing the best way to stage a kidnapping. When they reached the Marriott in Dahshur, there were too many people for them to execute it successfully. They would have to bide their time until the family was alone in their room. They parked across the street from the hotel and wandered into the bar area to wait.

Chapter 10:
At The Dig

Later that night, in our hotel room, I wrote:

Dear Journal,

Liam pulled another dangerous, stupid stunt. It was almost as heart-stopping as when he tried to jump off the roof. He snuck away in the back of the Bateses' truck to go on an adventure with him. We had to chase after him all the way to Dahshur. I was glad to see he was okay when we arrived at the Marriott in Dahshur, and Dad did well at keeping his composure. But I could tell he was angry and worried sick. The whole day went this way...

"Son, I am very disappointed in your behavior. You put yourself in unnecessary danger. What would have happened if you had gotten hurt? What would have happened to Mr. Bates if you had gotten hurt? You need to apologize to him right now and promise me you will never run off like this again."

Liam's head hung low as he listened to Dad. He looked at Mr. Bates and said, "I'm sorry, Mr. Bates; I promise never to hide in your truck again. Sorry, Dad."

"You're forgiven, Liam," said Bill. Turning to my dad, he added, "You know, Vic, we have extra tents, cots, and supplies. You and your family are welcome to join us as we explore the pyramids of Dahshur. They've discovered a 4,300-year-old tomb, and we've been invited to film them as they open it for the first time."

Liam's eyes sparkled with excitement. "Can we, Dad?"

My heart raced a hundred miles an hour. I prayed silently, saying, *Yes, Dad, please say yes.* I waited anxiously as Dad considered it.

He looked at Nana. "What do you think?"

"This would not only be a dream come true for Liam but for me too. When I was younger, I wanted to study archaeology, but life got in the way."

"Nana, did you want to be an archaeologist?" I asked.

"Yes, but I got married and had kids instead. I would love the opportunity to explore an ancient tomb, but I don't regret dedicating my life to my family either."

"Okay, Bill, it looks like we're staying the week with you. You'll have to put us to work to pay for our keep," Dad said.

Bill winked. "You got it, man. Liam, I'll teach you all about an archaeological dig."

Liam jumped up and down, squealing with excitement. I looked at Ben, who smiled back at me.

Once we settled into our rooms, we headed downstairs to the dining room and enjoyed a dinner of local dishes. We had bissara, a bean dip served with pita bread; falafel, which is like a fried bean pancake; and lamb shawarma, which is similar to a burrito. Everything was incredibly delicious. Afterward, we gathered in the lobby on the comfy couches, playing charades. Dad borrowed Bill's satellite phone, excused himself, and went to call his ship.

I noticed various people coming and going from the lobby. Most seemed to ignore us, but two outright stared at us, and not in a good way. I don't know why they felt the need to stare, and I tried not to stare back. I would glance over and see them, then glance away. It unnerved me, and I wondered if I should tell my dad or not. I decided against saying anything. Maybe they were just curious about the American tourist.

When Dad came back to the group, he looked upset. "Dad, is everything okay?" I asked.

"Sure," he said. "Bill, can I speak to you privately?" I was not reassured by this and wondered what Dad was keeping from me. I prayed that he wasn't being commanded to return to the ship and ruin our time together.

"I need to let you know about an incident that occurred on my ship just before I arrived," Vic said, and he explained to Bill about Amin, his threats, and his subsequent arrest. "I just found out from my second-in-command that Amin has escaped."

"What? How? When?"

"All they know is that he escaped while at the airport, and the authorities have been unable to find him. When they raided their hideout, it was abandoned. So no one was arrested."

"Vic, what are you going to do?"

"I guess I will continue with our plans and keep an extra eye out for trouble. I don't think Amin is stupid enough to try to follow through with his threats, but revenge is a significant motivator for some people."

Later that evening, in our room, I spent an hour texting Rachel about the wild adventure we were about to embark on. She was jealous and promised to tell Danny how Liam stowed away on Bill Bates's truck. He'd think that's hilarious.

When we finished, I laid down my phone and realized everyone else had fallen asleep. I checked my phone and saw that it was already midnight. I switched off my light and lay down next to Nana, when I heard a sound. I sat up and looked around, trying to identify what I was hearing. Then it dawned on me: Someone was turning the doorknob, trying to enter our room.

My heart raced as I started to scream. I covered my mouth to muffle the sound, not wanting to scare Liam or Nana. Slipping out of bed, I tiptoed over to Dad. "Dad, Dad," I said, shaking his arm.

He mumbled, "Huh, what, what's wrong, honey?"

"Someone's trying to get into our room," I whispered in a shaky voice.

Instantly, my dad was up and alert. As I climbed into his bed with Liam, he scanned the room for a weapon. The only thing he found was the table lamp, which he held over his right shoulder like a baseball bat as he approached the door. The doorknob turned slightly, but the lock held firm. Dad waited. After a few moments, he switched on the light, flipped the lock, and yanked the door open. Looking both ways, he saw that the hallway was empty.

He closed the door and locked it. He picked up the phone and reported the incident to the front desk. Then he returned to the bed, where I sat terrified. He wrapped his arms around me and assured me everything was alright; it was probably just a drunk who forgot his room number. I felt safe in his arms and sighed.

"It's been a crazy day, hasn't it, Dad?"

"Yes, it has."

I glanced at Liam and Nana, both snoring away, and shook my head. "I don't think even a train rumbling through the room would wake the two of them." My dad laughed, and we returned to bed. I slept well for the rest of the night.

But Victor O'Connor had trouble sleeping; every little noise made him jerk awake, ready to defend his family. He knew that somewhere out there, Amin was plotting his revenge—he could sense it. After an hour of restlessness, he prayed, and only then did he feel comfortable enough to go back to sleep.

###

The next day, we packed our things, joined the Bates team, and set off into the desert in several large trucks. I told Ben about the scare last night, and he seemed concerned.

"Are you alright?" he asked.

I nodded. "Yes, but it was scary. I'm glad my dad was there."

My dad informed Bill about the incident. "The

worst part was that I didn't have a weapon to use; I grabbed a lamp," he explained.

"Do you think it was Amin or just a simple mistake, someone entering the wrong room?" asked Bill.

"I don't know," Dad said, "But I was awake a lot last night."

"I can understand that. I hope Scotland Yard catches him soon."

The road was bumpy, and we were squeezed into the back seat like sardines in a can. We bounced around so much that I felt like a bobblehead doll. Finally, we arrived at base camp, dusty, dirty, and sweaty but filled with curiosity and excitement.

Meanwhile, a black car carrying Bahan and his companion followed the truck caravan. They stopped several miles away from the base camp, discreetly hiding their car behind a dune. The two men got out of the car and climbed to the top of the dune, where they used their binoculars to spy on the truck caravan.

One of the men pulled out his phone and talked to Amin. "We tried to get into their hotel room last night, but the lock held. Today, they drove to the pyramids along with the American explorer. They have now entered a restricted area around the pyramids. I believe a tomb is being excavated in that area, and there are armed guards. The closest option is the public parking lot, located approximately half a kilometer away. What should we do?”

Amin spat out several curse words before responding, “You two are useless. I will have to take care of this myself. Return to town and await my call. I will catch a flight as soon as possible.” The two men returned to their car and left.

We all looked around as we got out of the truck. The base camp had tents and equipment all around. An elderly Egyptian man approached our caravan, his hands outstretched and a broad smile on his face.

“Bill! Welcome, my friend. I’m so glad you made it.” He grabbed Bill’s hand and pumped it up and down.

“It’s great to see you, Dr. Hassan! Thank you so much for the invitation,” Bill said, gesturing to his team. Each man approached and shook hands with Dr. Hassan. At the same time, Bill introduced them, and then said, “And this is the O’Connor family, who decided to join us on this adventure: Captain Victor O’Connor, his mother Mary O’Connor, and his children, Cara and Liam.”

“Yes, welcome to all of you,” Dr. Hassan replied with a thick Egyptian accent, shaking hands with Dad.

136

"Dr. Hassan, the head of the Egyptian antiquities department, leads the investigation into this new discovery. We've collaborated on numerous projects over the past fifteen years," Bill explained.

"Yes, I'm a big fan of Bill's show. Excellent television! Come, let me show you the base camp." Dr. Hassan gestured for us to follow and he guided us around the camp, describing the various sections.

There was a dining tent large enough to seat about thirty people, used for group meetings; a tent for the kitchen; one for equipment storage; a tent where they cleaned and cataloged the artifacts they found; a medical tent for emergencies and illnesses; plus, portable latrines, a shower tent, and sleeping tents. There was also a roped-off area used to corral the camels.

Around the outer perimeter of the camp, armed guards patrolled. "Dr. Hassan, why are there armed guards here?" I asked.

"Ah, yes, you see, many people have heard of our discovery, and thieves may try to steal the artifacts during the night. Sometimes armed bandits have been known to storm a dig site and take off with everything, even the people."

Nana grew pale and looked at Dad.

"Um, I'm sure that doesn't happen if you have armed guards, right?" Dad asked, giving Nana a reassuring smile.

"No, no, here we are perfectly safe. Do not worry."

Nana still looked worried.

"Cara, look, camels!" Liam screamed as he ran toward them. He tried to coax the camels to approach him while we caught up. No matter how hard he tried and pleaded, they sat under the single shady palm tree, chewing their cud and not moving.

"Liam, later we shall ride the camels, but for now, I must show you the artifacts we found. Come, let me show you," Dr. Hassan said, taking Liam's hand.

Several workers were in the artifacts tent, cleaning, restoring, and tagging the pieces discovered in the tomb. Dr. Hassan described how the objects were used in ancient Egypt.

"Here, Cara, look, these pieces are from the same pot. Sabah is restoring this pot by carefully brushing away thousands of years of dust and dirt. Then, she will gently clean it with cotton swabs and glue it back together to make it whole again."

Sabah continued. "Yes, I love my work. Restoring this pot to its original state is like putting together a puzzle. Sometimes, it takes days or even weeks. When I finish, I will send it to my colleague Nuru to catalog and store until it's ready to display in the museum."

"In ancient Egypt, a girl of your age may have used this pot to carry water from the well to her home. Liam, maybe a boy your age would carry it, yes. Just like you, their mothers made them do housework, right?"

Liam nodded. "Except, it's my Nana and my big sister making me do chores because my mom is in heaven."

Dr. Hassan and Sabah looked sad. "I'm sorry for your loss," she said.

Dr. Hassan changed the subject, saying, "Come, I show you to your sleeping tents. You must put away your things and join us for lunch, okay?"

Our tent, constructed atop a wooden platform, accommodated the entire family. Inside were four cots outfitted with mattresses, blankets, pillows, a couple of folding chairs, and a small table beside each cot. A single electric light bulb hung from the center rafter. We left our bags on the cots and joined the others in the dining tent for lunch.

As we savored our lunch of beans, rice, and fruit, Dr. Hassan shared details about the latest tomb they had discovered.

"We were thrilled to discover a new tomb filled with artifacts, murals, and inscriptions. It is a cemetery from the Old Kingdom for the Dahshur community. What is notable about the findings is the details in the inscriptions that reveal their everyday activities. There are drawings from the deceased's life, such as harvesting grain, sailing on the Nile, buying and selling at the marketplace, and making offerings to their gods.

"This structure we are excavating is called a mastaba. It is an ancient rectangular tomb with sloping walls and a flat mudbrick or stone roof. The tombs feature deep shafts that lead to an underground burial chamber. We are discovering storage chambers filled with items intended for the afterlife, including pots, grain, jewelry, and many other artifacts."

"Dr. Hassan," Liam interrupted, "I've finished my lunch. May I give my apple core to the camels?"

Dr. Hassan smiled. "Ah, yes, very nice, Liam. Here, take all the apple cores and feed the camels. That will make you their favorite human."

Liam jumped up and began gathering cores from the table.

Ben said, "We'd better help him; his arms are too small to carry all that."

I nodded, and we assisted Liam with his rinds. "Besides, we want to keep an eye on his wanderings."

When the camels saw us coming, they all stood up and approached us for an apple core. Some snatched it right out of our hands, while others were wary and waited until we dropped it on the ground.

"Cara, I have a brilliant idea for pranking my dad. Liam, you can help," Ben said.

Liam was thrilled to be included, and I was all ears. "We'll need Dr. Hassan to help us because it involves camels. My dad hates camels and doesn't want to be near them."

"Ben, why does your dad hate camels? They're adorable."

"He's been bitten by them, spat on, kicked, and thrown off camels. They really don't like him. Maybe he smells funny to them, or maybe it's his red hair."

Just then, a local boy, a little older than Liam, appeared. "You have questions about camels? I have all the answers. I am Nasir."

Liam found a friend. "Hi, I'm Liam. I want to know all about camels. Do they like red hair? What else do they eat besides apple rinds? Can I pet one?"

"Camels can see some colors but not red. They mostly see desert colors. Yes, you can pet them. Here, I'll show you how to approach them."

"Hey, Ben," I whispered, "Let's let Liam hang out here with his new friend while you and I plan the prank."

As we walked away, I heard Nasir instructing Liam to hold his hand backward and slowly approach the camel. "Then he will sniff your hand and maybe sniff your head, too," Nasir said. "Only then should you slowly reach to pet him on his neck."

Liam followed Nasir's instructions and slowly approached one of the camels. The animal bent down, sniffing his hand and then his head. Liam giggled as the camel sniffed and tousled his hair, saying, "That tickles."

Finally, I was alone with Ben. We moved a few feet away and sat on a crate to discuss our plan to prank his dad while holding hands. We settled on a great prank and went to talk to Dr. Hassan. He loved the idea, and soon, we had everything ready to execute our prank.

First, we enlisted the cameraman, John. He stood outside, filming with his phone and trying hard not to laugh. Next, Dr. Hassan instructed several men to saddle and line the camels up in a row. Nasir and Liam helped. Then he called everyone to join him. He was taking them to see the new tomb.

Bill and the crew headed toward the trucks, but Dr. Hassan said, "Wait, you must choose a camel. There's no road where we're going, and the only way to get there is by camel."

John continued filming as Bill panicked. "What! Hassan, you know I hate camels! There must be another way to get there."

"Oh no, this is the only way. Too much sand for heavy trucks; come on, you'll see."

We all went over to the lined-up camels. One by one, we were taught how to mount a camel. Nana and I got on one, while Dad rode with Liam. We practiced using the reins, making the camels stop and go. We learned that to get them to kneel or stand, we should yell "Yit, yit, yit."

Bill stood off to the side with his arms crossed and a scowl on his face. Then Dr. Hassan offered him the reins of a camel. Bill looked at the reins, then at the camel, and then at Dr. Hassan, saying, "Nope, I'll walk."

Dr. Hassan smiled and asked, "Why do you hesitate, my friend? What's your problem with the camel, eh?"

"What you should be asking is what the camel's problem is with me. They bite me, spit on me, kick me, snarl at me, and generally hate me. I have no idea why."

"What's the hold-up, Dad?" Ben asked, sitting atop a camel. "Are you scared?"

Bill glared at him.

"Maybe you'd feel better after a few dad jokes. Why do camels blend so well into their surroundings? They use camel-flage!"

I laughed, but no one else did. Someone groaned, and John continued filming. I said, "Mr. Bates, what do you call a camel that cries? A humpback wail!"

Liam laughed. "How about this one—how can a camel cross the desert without getting hungry? Because there are plenty of sandwiches there."

"Okay, okay, I'll ride the monster camel. Just stop with the dumb dad jokes!"

Bill took the reins from Dr. Hassan and yelled, "Yit, yit, yit," but the camel refused to kneel. Instead, its ears went back, and it let out a horrible camel yell, then spit at Bill, who ducked just in time. "See, I told you camels hate me!"

"Well, Bill, you're in luck. The tomb is within walking distance. We only use camels to carry equipment," Dr. Hassan laughed. Everyone joined in the laughter—except Bill.

"Not funny," muttered Bill, handing the reins to Nasir.

"Yes, very funny," Nasir replied, still laughing.

"Yes, very funny," said John as he finished filming. Bill just glared while we all laughed.

"Gotcha!" said Ben.

"So, you're the one behind this," Bill said to his son. "Okay, watch out; I will plot my revenge." Then he smiled evilly.

Dr. Hassan said, "Come, everyone, let us go see the tomb of Neseb-Ben-Fa."

"Can we ride the camels there?" asked Liam.

"No, no camels!" yelled Bill.

"Aww," said Liam as we got off the animals.

The new tomb wasn't far, but walking through the sand and heat was exhausting. We all wore sunscreen, hats, and other protective clothing, yet I still felt as if I were burning. My mouth became so dry that I had to sip from my water bottle three times during the short distance. I wondered how a camel could survive a week in this environment without water.

The tomb was underground. A dirt ramp led up to an opening at the base of the pyramid, which a stone slab had once sealed. Inside, the temperature dropped by twenty degrees. It felt refreshing.

The crew filmed as we entered the tomb. Dr. Hassan guided us through, pointing out the drawings and carvings on the walls and explaining their significance to the individual buried there. Bill narrated each step and asked Dr. Hassan numerous questions about the life of Neseb-Ben-Fa.

I was fascinated by the beautiful colors on the wall. It was incredible to see the craftsmanship of the ancient artist.

We passed another opening that was roped off. "Dr. Hassan, where does this lead?" Liam asked, poking his head under the rope. His voice echoed down the empty corridor.

"That is a new shaft we have just uncovered. We haven't fully explored that area yet. We must take our time in each new section to identify and clear any potential traps or structural issues. We also add scaffolding and braces where necessary to reinforce the deteriorating ancient walls. You can never be too careful."

"They really built traps inside the tombs?" I asked.

"Yes, the Ancients built traps, false doors, and meandering corridors that lead nowhere to mislead tomb raiders and safeguard the treasures that accompanied them on their journey to the afterlife."

"Did they go to heaven?" Liam asked.

"They believed that after death they would reach the Field of Reeds if the gods allowed it. This can be viewed as their version of heaven."

Liam continued to stare down the roped-off corridor.

"Come on, Liam, we have so much more to explore," Dr. Hassan urged.

As we progressed, Liam asked, "Where is the Field of Reeds, and how do you get there?"

"Ah, good questions, my boy. The story goes like this: The ancient Egyptians believed that after death, the soul could reside forever in a paradise known as the Field of Reeds, which mirrored the life one had lived on earth. When a person died, their soul was thought to be trapped in the body. Spells, amulets, and images painted on tomb walls helped to guide the soul from the tomb to the Hall of Truth. We often find these items in tombs."

Dr. Hassan paused and pointed to the walls of the tomb. "Look here, Liam. See these paintings on this wall? This creature that resembles a man with a jackal head is Anubis, the guide of the dead, who accompanied the soul to this Hall of Truth. There, the soul would make the Negative Confessions before the gods Osiris, Thoth, and Anubis, and the Forty-Two Judges.

"The Negative Confessions were a list of sins that the soul had to honestly confess to never having committed, such as lying or stealing. If the soul's confession was accepted, it would present its heart to Osiris to be weighed on golden scales against the white feather of truth. If the heart was lighter than the feather, it signified that the soul was truthful, allowing it to proceed to the next phase of its journey to the Field of Reeds. However, if the heart was heavier, it indicated that the soul had lied and was cast to the ground, where Ammut devoured it. She is the goddess known as the devourer of the dead.

"The next stop on the path was Lily Lake, where it met the cruel Ferryman, Hraf-hef. There, the soul had to be very kind to him to continue its journey. If the soul passed this test, then Hraf-hef would carry it across the waters to the Field of Reeds in his boat. Here, it would find its deceased loved ones, favorite possessions, lost pets, and home, where it could enjoy eternity."

Dr. Hassan stopped at another opening. "Here we are. This is Neseb-Ben-Fa's tomb room. You have a remarkable opportunity to witness the opening of his sarcophagus for the first time. Bill and your crew need to film, yes? Come, I will lead the way. The rest of you can watch from here; the room is too small to accommodate everyone."

I pulled out my camera and filmed in night vision mode as Bill and his crew followed Dr. Hassan. They descended a ladder into a small chamber where a massive sarcophagus sat in the middle. The men positioned the cameras and lights while Bill narrated. We stood crowded around the door, peering in and waiting with anticipation.

"Okay, men, push," said Dr. Hassan as he leaned into the heavy stone lid. All the crew and Bill pushed along with him, and the lid shifted halfway.

"Again." They pushed hard once more, and the top shifted enough to reveal a second intricately decorated wooden sarcophagus inside. The crew heaved the stone top aside and onto the floor, then lifted the lid from the inner wooden sarcophagus, unveiling the mummy.

"Look at this! The mummy remains here, completely undamaged. Neseb-Ben-Fa's welcome to the twenty-first century," Bill exclaimed.

It was both fascinating and horrifying. The mummy, with its dried, shriveled flesh and deathly grimace, was terrible to behold, but the fact that it was over four thousand years old and had survived intact all this time was astonishing.

"Since the body is still intact, does this mean the grave robbers never discovered this tomb?" asked Bill.

"Yes, no one has seen this body. The outer parts of the tomb were robbed, and items were taken, but this chamber was so well hidden that it remained unopened. It is indeed a very rare find. We had to use Lidar."

"You mean that radar device that detects things hidden underground?" asked Ben.

Bill nodded.

"That's dope, Dad."

"Can someone use Lidar to find the way to the Field of Reeds, too?" suggested Liam. Everyone laughed. Liam looked confused because he was serious. He sighed. "Never mind," he muttered to himself.

The men covered the mummy again to protect it from the elements. Then, we marched back to the base camp, where each of us went off to engage in different activities around the camp.

Sabah came out to greet us as we returned. I took Sabah's arm and walked off to join her in her work. As we walked, she whispered to me about her secret crush on one of the young men working in the tomb. We giggled a lot, and Ben grew nervous, thinking we were talking about him.

Liam enjoyed using the sand sifter. This device involved dumping a shovel full of sand onto a series of screens and moving those screens back and forth, sifting the sand through the holes until shards of pottery or other small objects were revealed. This method prevented the tiniest pieces from being lost and allowed them to be reattached to the objects they broke off from, completing their restoration.

Nana liked helping the cook and learning about Egyptian cuisine. Dad stayed busy assisting the men in digging and moving artifacts to the restoration tent. Bill and his crew filmed or edited their project. Part of his team flew the drone over the pyramid, capturing the beautiful scenery. Ben stayed close to me, helping wherever he could. By the end of the day, we were all exhausted but felt accomplished.

As dusk drew near, Bill spoke to Vic. "Should you let Dr. Hassan know what happened last night? Maybe tell him the whole story about Amin?"

"What happened last night? And who is Amin?" asked Dr. Hassan.

Vic looked around to see who was listening before answering. "Dr. Hassan, just before I came to London, I escorted a traitor from my ship to England for prosecution. He threatened to harm my family if I didn't let him go. After I handed him over to the authorities, he escaped, and I'm worried he's after us for revenge. Last night, someone tried to enter our room while we were sleeping."

"Oh, this is terrible. We will need to take precautions. I have armed guards stationed near the tomb, and we will also have some posted around the sleeping tents."

"Thank you, that would make me feel much better."

Later that evening, as we chatted around the campfire, Liam whispered, "Sis, do you think we can go back to the tomb tomorrow? I want to sneak a peek down that new shaft."

"I can't believe this! Didn't you hear the adults say it was unsafe and warn you not to go down there? Liam, you must stay near the artifacts tent and not wander off. The desert is no place to get lost, and you should stay away from that shaft. You enjoyed sifting sand; do that tomorrow, or feed the camels, but please don't march off on another misadventure!"

Liam huffed in frustration, then stomped to the other side of the campfire and plopped down next to his new friend Nasir in the sand. I couldn't hear their conversation, but I could tell he was unhappy with me since they kept glancing back at me.

"Oh, oh, looks like steam is coming from Liam's ears again. Who's he mad at now?" Ben asked.

"It's me. Always me. But I don't even care. He wanted to check out that new shaft in the tomb."

"Man, he really knows how to pick 'em, doesn't he?"

The next day, I watched Liam like a hawk. I didn't want a repeat of the incident in the cornfield. It seemed like Liam was done with the idea of investigating the new shaft; he was having a blast with Nasir. They spent most of their time caring for the camels. However, they did get into trouble for holding an unauthorized camel race.

One of the Egyptian workers rushed by our tent, yelling something in Arabic, flailing his arms as if a bird were attacking him while looking over his shoulder. I heard what sounded like distant thunder and stepped out of the artifact tent with my phone in hand to see what was going on.

I was filming when the worker dashed past, and a few seconds later, two squawking camels came hurtling by, one with Nasir and the other with Liam shouting "Yeehaw" as they chased after the worker.

Right behind them was Dr. Hassan yelling, "Liam, Nasir, you must not race the camels."

The entire camp erupted in laughter at the scene. They continued racing, disregarding Dr. Hassan, until the camels had had enough and abruptly halted, causing both boys to tumble into the sand. Fortunately, they weren't hurt, and as they got up and brushed off the sand, Dr. Hassan lectured them on the importance of listening and following instructions.

To Nasir, he yelled in Arabic, "*Nasir! mae khatbak ya chup! ant chaki jedda.*"

Then he repeated the same message to Liam in English: "Liam! What's the matter with you, young man? You're being very naughty."

I was cracking up. I downloaded the video along with the text to Rachel: *Make sure to show this to Danny!* She replied with a message full of laughing, rolling-on-the-floor emojis.

I shared the video with Nana, Dad, and the rest of the gang, and we all roared with laughter. Nana suggested we submit it to *America's Funniest Videos*.

###

As the week flew by, Ben and I had plenty of time to talk while working alongside the Egyptian archaeologist and their team. Additionally, Bill's crew provided us with valuable insights on editing, filming, and flying the drone.

Liam seemed to forget about the restricted shaft. He and Nasir set up targets made of empty boxes and cans to practice hitting with the whip. They resembled two mini-me's of Indiana Jones.

But the most magical experience came when the lights went out at night. Then, we could see the stars—millions of them, clusters of stars and galaxies visible to the naked eye, along with the largest moon I've ever seen. It took our breath away. There were no words. It made me want to worship the Lord God Almighty. It was time to find out if Ben and I shared the same beliefs. Were we equally yoked? *Please let it be yes, Jesus.*

"Ben, do you believe in God?" I asked as we sat beneath the starry sky.

"How can you not when you see this?" he replied, pointing upward. "But I'm not sure He gets involved in our lives."

"I believe He does. My family attends a full Gospel church, which means we believe that everything the Bible says is the truth, not just made-up stories. We believe the only way to heaven is by accepting Jesus as our Lord and Savior. His sacrifice on the cross covers our sins.

"I've been contemplating the Egyptian story of the afterlife, which describes being judged by Osiris and answering forty-two questions. Imagine standing before God and having to account for your actions, both good and bad, throughout your life. Could you answer yes to all the questions? I recall stealing a pencil from the store once. I felt so guilty that I returned it, but now I see myself as a thief. Additionally, how many lies have I told? I still make mistakes like that; I mean, come on, I snuck out to a bar with you. Only Jesus lived a sinless life.

"When I was ten, before my mom passed away, I gave my heart to Jesus, and now I follow His guidance in my life. When I make mistakes, I ask for His forgiveness. I can't express how much of a difference Jesus has made in my life. I feel so much peace now. The Bible describes it as 'the peace that surpasses all understanding.' I really like you, Ben, and I wanted to share my thoughts."

Ben was silent for a moment. "I appreciate you sharing that with me. I remember going to my grandfather's church when I was little, before my mom and I moved to California. I loved hearing the Bible stories and singing the songs in church. I believe Jesus was a great man, but I'm uncertain about the other points you mentioned. I will reflect on it."

I wasn't sure how to feel about that response, but it was a start.

Meanwhile, at Cairo Airport, Amin walked out to join Bahan and his driver. He hopped into their car, and they drove off to spy on the camp.

Chapter 11:
Cave-In

The next day, we were all busy with various tasks when a worker burst into the camp, shouting something in Arabic. He ran straight to Dr. Hassan, and before long, they embraced and shared a laugh. Turning to the rest of the camp, he exclaimed, "We found it! We've discovered the tomb room of Deti, Neseb-Ben-Fa's wife." Everyone erupted into joyous cheers.

"Come, let's take a look. Bill, grab your camera."

Everyone scrambled to gather their gear and raced toward the tomb. Ben and I followed the rest of the crew, bringing up the rear.

As we passed the closed shaft marked with tape, I noticed Nasir sitting beside it, waiting patiently. I stopped and stared at Nasir. Something felt off about this scene.

I looked at Ben and pointed to Nasir. "I need to ask him something."

I walked back to Nasir. His eyes widened with fear, and he hunched down to appear smaller. Ben stayed close to me, curious about what was happening. "Nasir, where's Liam? I thought you two were hanging out together."

Nasir wouldn't make eye contact. "How should I know? He's somewhere—maybe Allah knows, but I do not."

I glared at him. "Stop trying to cover for him and tell me!"

Nasir jumped up and pointed to the shaft. "I tell him not go down there, but he no listen. He say stay here and yell if someone come. But everyone come at once, and I was scared I get in trouble, so I stay quiet."

"Oh snap! He did it again, Ben. Liam went down the closed shaft on another adventure. What are we gonna do?"

Ben replied, "First, don't panic. Let's go in after him and try to get him out before he gets hurt. Nasir, stay here. If anything goes wrong or you hear a crash or screaming, go get help. "

Nasir nodded.

Ben grabbed Nasir's flashlight while I turned on my phone's light. We removed the safety ropes and entered the new shaft, with Ben leading the way. The shaft was dark, but we could see thanks to the illumination from our devices. Beautiful artwork adorned the clay brick walls, but we didn't stop to examine it. Debris littered the floor, left untouched by the crew, so we had to watch our step.

With no permanent lighting, the bugs scurried everywhere as soon as the light touched them. I was so busy dodging the creepy crawlies that I didn't think to call out for Liam. Soon, we reached an intersection with two paths.

"Which way should we go?" Ben asked.

"I'm not sure, hold on. Liam!" I shouted. There was no response.

"Liam, answer us!" yelled Ben. Still no answer.

"Crap! Okay, let's take the right; I don't think we should split up; it's too dangerous," I said. Ben agreed.

I was too scared to feel angry at Liam. What if he fell into a deep pit? What if Ben and I fell into a deep pit? Maybe we would trip a booby trap and be stuck here forever. Maybe the walls would cave in.

We continued down the shaft in silence, carefully picking our way. In some areas, the ceiling was too low, forcing us to bend down. Finally, we rounded a corner and reached the end of the shaft.

Ben sighed. "Sorry, Cara, this is the end and no Liam. Let's head back the other way."

We turned around, and I took the lead. When we returned to the intersection, I marched down the left side. "Liam!" I yelled. Nothing—not even crickets.

It felt eerie in this place. The only living things we encountered were occasional spiders and insects. The left side featured more wall art and hieroglyphics.

Then we rounded another corner, and there was Liam, flashlight in hand, inspecting a section of the wall. He was so engrossed that he didn't hear us approach.

"Liam!" I snapped.

Startled, Liam jumped, exclaiming, "Cara, you scared me to death!"

"You're in serious trouble, mister! Now get your hiney up and march outside, where you'd better prepare for the longest grounding you've ever had! You lied to Dad. You said you would never go on another misadventure, and here you are, breaking your word."

"I didn't lie!"

"You did, too! He made you promise not to go on any more misadventures, and you said, 'I promise.'"

"I said I'd never sneak into Mr. Bates's truck again, and I haven't. I never promised not to go on a misadventure."

I stopped and looked at him. Reflecting on our conversation, I realized he was right. Man, he's a tricky little guy. You almost had to admire him.

"Listen, buster, I don't care about that anymore. You need to get moving before something bad happens. March!" I got behind him and gave him a little shove.

"Hey, cut it out!"

"Shut up!"

Ben just rolled his eyes as we argued, but at least we were heading in the right direction. Liam mumbled and complained as we went until suddenly, he tripped on something and fell to the floor, scraping his knee.

"Ouch, that hurt," he said as he got back up. He must have stepped on some sort of trap release because we all heard a loud click.

A slight rumble came from somewhere. We all froze in place. The rumble grew louder, and dust and small rocks began to rain down on us.

"It's a cave-in!" yelled Ben. "Run!"

We ran toward the entrance of the main shaft. We were almost there when we noticed the opening becoming smaller.

"What's happening?" I yelled.

"The opening is closing up. We've got to hurry!" Ben shouted.

We were almost there. I could see we weren't going to make it. The opening was nearly shut, and I pushed Liam through; then I fell, debris raining down on me. Instinctively, I covered my head and curled into a ball, and then everything went black...

Liam fell through to the other side. He rolled along the dirt floor and slammed into a wall. Dirt and debris fell all around him. He was terrified, unable to speak due to the pollutants in the air. He covered his head and waited for it to end, wondering if he would die. Tears ran down his face, leaving streaks through the dirt.

"Cara!" he tried to yell, but the dust choked him, forcing him to cough instead. He began to pray in his head: *Jesus, help me! Help my sister!*

Then everything fell silent. He lay still for a few moments before raising his head and scanning the surroundings. Everything was black; he could see nothing. He began to scream. He called out for Cara, then his dad, then his nana, and everyone else he could remember. He shouted for help until his voice was raw. Sitting on the ground, he hugged his legs to himself, sobbing and waiting for someone to rescue him. "Jesus, help me. Jesus, forgive me."

I was dreaming. I had that same dream earlier in the week. I was riding a camel in the desert, with the pyramids in the background, but the camel kept stumbling over rocks. Then I found myself surrounded by dark water; I was being pulled under, and my heart raced, but I couldn't call out for help. Just as I was about to drown, a hand reached down and pulled me out. There was a voice this time: "Cara, Cara, wake up."

"Jesus, is that you? Where am I?"

"Cara, Liam needs you."

I woke up to the sound of my little brother screaming my name. He sounded frantic. My brain was foggy; I didn't know where I was. It felt like being in a dream. I tried to clear my head and remember what had happened.

Panic started to rise within me. Where am I? Where's Liam? Is he all right? What's happening? I felt a weight pressing down on me. I opened my eyes, but everything was black. It was so dark that I couldn't tell if my eyes were open.

I blinked a few times, causing my head to throb. Wow, the headache I had was intense. I still couldn't see anything. This kind of darkness seeps into your bones, making you feel like you're the last person on earth. I shuddered.

I reached out, feeling my surroundings. I was lying on a sandy floor, with rocks and debris scattered around me. In the distance, I could hear my little brother sobbing. I brushed off some debris and attempted to stand on my shaky legs, but there wasn't enough space, so I sat down and leaned back against a cold brick wall. I coughed and spat sand out of my mouth.

I could no longer hear Liam. I felt dazed. The only sound reaching my ears was the pounding of my heart. I touched my arms, face, and body, checking for injuries. I was bloody, cut up, and sore, but I couldn't find any broken bones, just soreness.

I brushed off the remaining dust and debris from my clothes and leaned back to catch my breath. The adrenaline was fading, and I began to feel a lot more pain. My whole body ached, and I was shivering. I pulled my knees up to my chest and wrapped my arms around myself to keep warm. I felt grimy and was coughing and hacking from the dust in the air.

I heard a moan in the darkness and panicked, letting out a shriek. Someone was in here with me. Who or what made that sound? Where were they? What happened? I tried to remember. I heard the other person moan again and cough, choking on the dusty air.

Suddenly, it all came back to me. There had been a cave-in. I was inside an ancient pyramid. Liam had been next to me when the cave-in occurred. I had pushed him out of the way just before the wall collapsed. Ben had also been with me. I felt around the space, calling his name.

"Ben! Ben, are you alright?"

Ben moaned. "I-I think so. What happened? Where are we?"

"There was a cave-in. We're stuck in the shaft, but Liam made it out. I heard him on the other side of this wall. Liam! Liam!" I screamed hysterically.

I couldn't hear him. I was terrified that he had been crushed by falling debris. My lips began to quiver, and tears made streaks through the dirt on my face. "Liam!"

I heard his voice coming from the outer wall. "Cara, are you and Ben okay?"

I leaned in close and yelled, "Yes, we're okay. Are you alright?"

"Yeah, I'm okay." I could hear him crying. "I'm sorry."

"Liam, stop crying and look around. Do you see a way out?"

"Yeah, I see some daylight through a gap in the wall."

"Can you get through it?"

"Yeah, I think so."

"Then go get the adults. Go get help; I'm stuck in here."

"I don't want to leave you!"

"There's nothing you can do; you need to get the adults. I'll be fine; go now."

I should have been angry with him. I told him not to touch anything, to stay in the artifacts tent, and not to go down the new shaft they had uncovered in the pyramid, but he never listened. It was always about the next great adventure with him. But I was so relieved he was alive. Knowing he was safe and not trapped with Ben and me was comforting.

Ben and I had gone down the shaft after him, but hadn't expected a booby trap. I could feel tears welling up in my eyes again; I sobbed uncontrollably.

"Don't cry, Cara. My dad will rescue us."

I felt around in the blackness looking for my cell phone. When I found it, I could feel that the screen was shattered. I turned it on, but it was ruined. I couldn't make a call, but I had a little light. I shone it around the area. We were in a small rectangular space with a sandy floor strewn with rocks and debris. I couldn't see an exit, no light coming through.

Ben was lying beside me. His head was bloodied, and a large stone pinned his leg.

"Oh, Ben, your leg," I said, pointing.

He glanced down and then reclined again. "Look for a lever to lift the stone."

I set my phone against a rock to light up the area. I scanned around and spotted a piece of timber, which I wedged under the stone, pinning Ben's leg. I pushed hard, but it didn't move.

"Get a fulcrum, a rock, or anything to place under the lever to gain leverage," Ben said.

I wedged a rock under the lever and pushed with all my might. It shifted slightly, allowing Ben to slide his leg out, gasping from the pain of his efforts. He sat up with his back against the brick wall. I sat beside him, and we huddled together, a sliver of light coming from my broken phone.

"Is your leg alright?"

"I think it's broken or badly sprained."

Ben spat and coughed, "My mouth is full of sand and dust. Is there any water?"

I picked up the phone, shone the light around, trying to find the bottle of water, my backpack, anything. I saw my pack under some rubble and dug it out. Thank God the water bottle inside was undamaged.

"Here," I said as I lifted the bottle to Ben's lips. He sat up, took a big swig, and swallowed, followed by a lot of coughing. "Careful, now, just a sip at a time. We don't know how long this water will have to last us."

He sat back, breathing hard, and nodded. I took a small sip and ran it around my mouth, swallowing the dirt.

"I'm so sorry. This is why we call Liam's mischief misadventures," I muttered.

Ben snickered. "Yeah, Liam really knows how to have fun, doesn't he?" He grimaced in pain.

It was getting colder, and I began to shiver. I dug my feet into the sand beneath me, which felt warmer than the air. "It's getting cold. Maybe if we cover ourselves with sand, we'll stay warm until help arrives."

"I believe our body heat will be more effective. Come, snuggle closer to me." Ben pulled me into his embrace, making me feel warm and safe in his arms. I rested my head on his shoulder, and tears started to flow again.

###

On the other side of the wall, Liam's eyes adjusted to the dark, and he saw a small sliver of light. He moved toward it, crawling over debris, and began to dig his way out, shifting rocks and brushing away dirt. The hole gradually grew larger, allowing him to stick his hand through. He dug some more, determined to escape and save his sister. His hands were bloody, scraped, and in pain, but he pressed on.

He heard someone on the other side; a whisper reached him. "Liam, my friend, is that you? Are you alright?" It was Nasir.

"Nasir, help me. Help me dig this hole bigger so I can get out." The two boys dug for a while, but then they encountered large boulders that they couldn't move.

"I will go and get the adults," said Nasir. Liam nodded. As Nasir ran off to get help, Liam turned around and sat down to wait. His body shook from the exertion of digging, and he cradled his hands against his chest, now feeling pain coursing through him. He sniffled and fought hard to hold back his tears.

###

We were quiet for a while, and then Ben asked, "So, have there been any misadventures worse than this one?"

"Plenty! In fact, I have written many of them in my journal. Someday, I will make a book about all his misadventures. Once, he tied a towel around his neck and declared he was Superman. Some workmen had left a ladder leaning against the house. He climbed up onto the roof and was going to jump, convinced he could fly. As always, I had to come to his rescue and talk him down before he hurt himself.

"It was the first time I remember him attempting one of his misadventures. It was a year after my mom died, and he was only five years old. He kept saying he had someplace to go. If he got there, we would all be happy. I never understood what he meant, but he said something like that after every foolish misadventure he tried. Once, I asked him what that meant, but he muttered that I wouldn't understand."

"Wow! You are a good sister." Ben said, "I'm getting really tired; maybe we should conserve energy and stop talking."

"Okay, but I think you may have a concussion, and I've heard you shouldn't go to sleep. So I'm going to make sure you stay awake."

Ben nodded, and we held each other in silence. Our only light slowly faded as my cell phone battery died. Once it blinked out, we sat in the dark, straining to hear any sound of workers digging to get us out.

But all we heard was silence.

Once my eyes adjusted to the darkness, I noticed a sliver of light coming from somewhere.

"Ben, didn't you have a flashlight?"

"Yeah, it's here somewhere; dig around. Maybe you'll find it."

I felt around in the dark and finally located the flashlight, still on and half buried in the sand. I dug it out and shone it around the room looking for an exit.

"What are you doing?"

"Looking for another exit." I shone the flashlight up and down and realized there was an opening, like a doorway, beyond the debris and rocks. "Ben, there's another opening over here. I'm gonna move some of these rocks and see what's on the other side."

"Okay, but be careful; we don't need any more booby traps to go off."

I began digging and moving rocks, and the opening grew large enough to crawl through. I pushed my head and arm in and looked around with the flashlight. I couldn't believe what I was seeing. I retracted my arm and head and turned back to Ben.

"Um, Ben, I think I've found another tomb chamber with a sarcophagus in it."

"What! You've got to be kidding! That would be amazing. We should definitely tell Dad and Dr. Hassan when they come to get us out."

"Well, I can't see clearly, and I wanna make sure that's what it is, so I'm goin' in there to check it out."

"Oh no, Cara, don't, it's too dangerous."

But I had already crawled through. I could hear Ben calling me back, but I had to find out what this place was. Once inside, I slowly stood up. I didn't bump my head, so the ceiling was high enough. Then, I carefully shone the flashlight around the room.

I was awed. Inside, there were the most beautiful hieroglyphics, with bright colors on the walls and ceiling. In the middle of the room was a small sarcophagus on a platform. Dust covered everything, and a strong, musty odor filled the air. I must have been the first person to enter here in thousands of years.

This must have been what it was like for Bill Bates and Dr. Hassan. Discovering such a treasure was thrilling. At that moment, I felt I could be an explorer.

I walked over to the sarcophagus, and it was so small I realized it must belong to a child. My heart sank. Suddenly, I felt the grief of the child's parents as they laid their child inside this dark place. Their only hope was that he or she would find their way to the Field of Reeds. I laid my hand on the stone and wept.

I wish I could have been here to give the parents better hope, to tell them about the true God and heaven, to reassure them that their child was with

Him now and was happy. I wish I could have comforted them in their grief; I understood grief.

"Cara, are you alright? I hear you crying."

"I'm okay, Ben," I sobbed. "It's a child's tomb. I have discovered a child's tomb."

I wiped my eyes and returned to Ben's side. I leaned my head on his shoulder while he wrapped his arms around me. We sat together in silence for a long time; the only sound was the rhythm of our own hearts.

Nasir ran off to tell Dr. Hassan and the other adults to come quickly and bring shovels. "Hurry, they are trapped!" Everyone grabbed a tool and ran after Nasir toward the new shaft.

Once they reached it, Dr. Hassan ordered Nasir to run back to camp and sound the alarm bell to gather more hands to dig out the kids. He ran quickly to the dining tent where a large bell hung on one of the poles. He pulled on the bell rope, causing it to ring repeatedly. Everyone in the camp came running, including Nana.

Nasir explained what was happening, and everyone grabbed a tool, basket, or wheelbarrow and ran toward the cave-in.

Watching through binoculars, Amin and his

companions knew something was wrong as the gates to the camp were thrown open and even the guards ran toward the dig site, laying down their weapons as they went.

An evil grin spread across Amin's face. "Allah be praised! There must have been a cave-in. Allah has made a way for us to enter the camp without a fight." He turned and grabbed his backpack. "Come, let us go straight in and find a discreet place to hide until night; then we will take the O'Connors."

Amin and his companions sprinted across the desert and through the open gates, choosing a tent filled with crates packed with artifacts, which were prepared to be shipped to the Museum of Antiquities. They settled down to wait for dark, making themselves as comfortable as possible while sitting on the floor behind the crates. They had water and dried food, as well as weapons in case they needed to fight their way out.

Bahan asked Amin, "There are three of us and four of them; how shall we all fit in our sedan?"

Amin pondered this before responding. "For once in your life, Bahan, you have asked a good question." Bahan smiled.

"I considered cramming the captain into the trunk, but we still have the issue of too many people. We must leave someone behind, perhaps the grandmother, or we steal one of the trucks out there," Amin explained. "I will go now while everyone is busy with the rescue and see if any of the trucks have keys in them."

Amin peeked out from the tent flap. The area was clear of people, so he hunched down and ran from the tent to the nearest truck. He quietly opened the door and climbed in. He searched every cavity he could for a set of keys but didn't find any. He continued to the next truck and then the next. Four trucks later, he found a set of keys. He stuffed them in his pocket and went back to wait for nightfall. He smiled as he anticipated victory over his arch-enemy, Vic O'Connor.

Chapter 12:
Liam's Secret

Liam heard the rescuers coming, so he yelled, "Over here! Help us!"

Vic was the first to reach him. "Liam, son, are you alright?"

"Dad, I'm okay. But Cara and Ben are stuck behind a wall of bricks and junk. You've got to help them." Liam began to sob.

"It's okay, son. We're here now. Stay back from the hole as we dig you out first."

From behind the crowd of workers, Nana's frantic voice yelled, "Liam, Cara, Vic, where are you? Is everyone okay?"

"Nana, there was a cave-in," yelled Liam.

"Mom, they're alive, but stuck behind debris. We're working on digging them out now."

The workers were familiar with cave-ins, and as Dr. Hassan barked orders, they lined up along the corridors. Some began passing rocks and debris back toward the tomb's entrance. They passed large rocks hand over hand to a wheelbarrow waiting outside the tomb, then moved them away, dumped them into the desert, and ran back for another load.

Others used shovels to remove dirt and smaller rocks from the entrance, placing them in large baskets that were carried away and dumped outside or transferred to wheelbarrows for transport from the tomb.

Once the opening was big enough for him to fit through, Liam squeezed through and tumbled down the rocks and debris that had piled up on the other side. As he did, he felt strong arms scoop him up. His dad set him on the ground and quickly checked him over, brushing off the dirt from his face. "Son, are you all right?" Liam nodded, but his body shook uncontrollably.

Dad wiped away his tears. "Okay, calm down, son. It's going to be okay. Oh, your hands; they're covered in blood."

"Never mind that, Dad; save Cara, please!"

Nana made her way through the crowd until she reached Liam and hugged him tightly. "I'll take him back to camp and tend to his wounds," she said to Vic.

"Good idea; take Nasir with you."

"I want to help my sister," yelled Liam.

"Me too," said Nasir.

"Boys, there are already too many people in here. You'll just get in the way. Go on now." The boys hung their heads but went with Nana obediently.

Bill and his crew quickly broke through the first blockage and shouted to Ben and Cara on the other side of the second wall. They only heard muffled sounds. They continued to work, removing debris until they reached the second wall, behind which were Cara and Ben.

"Cara, Ben, can you hear me? How are you two doing in there?" asked Bill.

"We hear you. We're okay, but looking forward to getting out of here," replied Ben.

"Mr. Bates," Cara yelled, "There's another tomb in here."

"What? Another tomb? Dr. Hassan, did you hear that? Who could it be? Since we have the owner of the pyramid and his wife's tomb, who is left?"

"Dr. Hassan," Cara said. "It's a child's tomb."

Everyone was silent. Finally, Dr. Hassan replied quietly, "It must be their son or daughter. We discover so many mummies and tombs that we sometimes need to be reminded these were families, and we are uncovering their grief."

Bill and some others nodded in agreement, and

then everyone returned to digging and breaking through the wall. Suddenly, a lot of dust and pebbles began to rain down, and Dr. Hassan yelled, "Stop."

No one moved an inch until the dust settled. "This area must be unstable. We need to reinforce the sides and ceiling with beams before we continue." He barked some orders to his men in Arabic, and off they ran to get the necessary equipment. Everyone else sat down to wait.

Vic turned to the wall to let the kids know what was happening. "Kids, we've had to stop digging until we can reinforce the walls and ceilings. How are you doing? Can you describe your injuries?"

"I'm fine, Dad," said Cara. "Just minor scratches and bruises. But I think Ben has a concussion and maybe a broken leg."

"Alright, we're coming as soon as possible. Try to keep Ben alert and awake."

"Already on it!"

It was quiet for a while as we waited. After a moment of silence, I asked, "Ben, how are you doing?"

No answer. "Ben, Ben," I yelled, and shook him gently.

"Huh, um, ya... sorry. I guess I dozed off."

"Ben, stay awake. Remember you have a concussion."

"Hum, no, just five more minutes."

"No! Ben, wake up," I said, shaking him gently and sitting him up straight. "Tell me a dad joke; you have got to stay awake."

"Okay, okay. Um... I can't think of any. You tell me a joke."

"Um, okay, here's one of Nana's favorite jokes. What do you call a cow with no legs?"

"I dunno."

"Ground beef."

No answer, then a slight chuckle.

"That was pretty good, tell me another."

"Um, let me think... okay, what do you call a dog with no legs?"

"I dunno, what?"

"Doesn't matter, he ain't comin'."

That got a laugh and a moan of pain from Ben. "Don't make me laugh, it hurts."

"But they say laughter is the best medicine. What do you call a cat with four good legs? Doesn't matter. He ain't comin' either."

Ben chuckled and then went into a coughing fit. I pounded him on the back. He slowly stopped and was wheezing. "I'm okay, but no more jokes. I can't take laughing."

"Okay, just don't die on me; you're the first boy I ever loved." I slapped my hand over my mouth. *What did I just say? Jesus, help me. Tell me Ben didn't hear that.*

"So, you love me, eh?"

Dang those Vulcan ears. "Um, did I say that? Well, you know Christians are supposed to love all people, and I… um. Fine, I guess I love you."

Ben drew me to him and kissed my dirty head. "Yeah, I love you too."

I smiled and snuggled into him, and we quietly waited for our rescuers.

Our rescuers resumed their work, but hours passed. The dust in the room settled, making breathing slightly easier. I had to keep waking Ben up. I knew he must have been in a lot of pain because every time he moved, he moaned, yet he never complained. I felt filthy and experienced some pain too, but I could manage it.

"So, surfer dude, do you ever enter competitions?"

"Sometimes. It depends on where they are."

"You know the oldest surfing competition in the world is about an hour from my house."

"Are you talking about the East Coast Surfing Championship in Virginia Beach? You live that close to Virginia Beach?"

I nodded. "I bet my dad would let you stay with us if you behave."

"That would be awesome. Plus, I could come down from Boston University in the summer, which is much closer than California. Do you think he'll let me stay all summer and maybe get a job?"

"I think I can arrange that."

"Wait a minute. Your dad hates me. He might even kill me in my sleep."

I laughed. "Don't worry, I'll protect you. Hey, we could go to Busch Gardens; you'll love it! Oh, I can take you to church so you can meet my friends. Rachel already knows all about you."

"Who is Rachel?"

"Oh, just a friend who is totally jealous of our relationship. I've been texting her and sending her pictures of you."

"Hum, is she pretty?"

I punched him in the arm. "Never mind if she's pretty."

"Ouch, my arm! Okay, I'll stop. No more punching."

After what seemed like hours, a pick came through the wall along with a sliver of light. Hands dug into the wall from the other side, and an excited voice shouted, "We're through! I see them. Ben, Cara, are you okay?"

"Yeah, but boy, are we glad to see you guys," said Ben.

"I'm okay, but I don't think Ben can walk on his leg," I said.

The crew continued digging around the opening until it was large enough for me to crawl through. My dad grabbed me as soon as he could and hugged me tightly. "Dad, I'm okay, just sore and dirty; help Ben."

Then they turned and helped pull Ben through and laid him on a stretcher. They carried him into the medical tent, where Liam, Nana, and Nasir waited for us.

Ben and his dad went behind a curtain stretched across the tent, where Ben could be thoroughly examined. I sat on a cot while medics cleaned and bandaged my wounds.

We anxiously waited for the medical staff to examine Ben. After what seemed like an eternity, Bill emerged and said, "Ben is fine. He has a concussion and a severely sprained leg, not broken, and he will have to stay in the medical tent and rest for the next couple of days."

Everyone let out a sigh of relief.

Dad turned to face Liam. My breath caught in my throat as I realized he had to confront his mischievous spirit once and for all. He bent down to look Liam in the eye.

"Do you know how much trouble you've caused!" he yelled.

Liam stared at his feet, looking sad. Nana had

cleaned him up and bandaged his wounds. He fought back tears. His nose began to run, and he swiped it with his shirt sleeve since both hands were bandaged. He nodded.

I looked at Liam and saw angry adults surrounding him. The crew, Bill, Dad, and even the local workers stood around Liam with their arms crossed, scowling. I suddenly felt sorry for my little brother. A maternal instinct surged within me to wrap my arms around him and protect him from what was to come. But I didn't move. I knew Liam was about to receive the scolding of his life. There was no way to shield him from the consequences of his actions. My heart ached for him, but I understood he had to change his ways, and this might be the catalyst for doing so.

"Why, son, why do you insist on going on these misadventures? You constantly put yourself and, often, your sister in danger. You upset your family, and now Ben is hurt. You have to stop doing these things."

"I can't stop!" sobbed Liam. "Everyone is still so sad. Cara is sad, Nana is sad, you're sad, I'm sad. We can't be happy unless I find it!" Everyone looked at one another, confused by Liam's words.

I knelt to look him in the eyes and asked, "Liam, what are you trying to find?"

He wiped his sleeve across his eyes and nose. "Heaven. That's what the man said at her funeral, remember? He said that Mom was on a new adventure in heaven. If I go on an adventure, maybe I can find heaven, and then Mom can come back, and we will be happy again."

I was floored. The funeral had been so long ago, and I didn't think he understood anything that happened that day. For the first time, I realized what a struggle Liam was going through. It never occurred to me that he even remembered Mom; he was barely four when she died. All these years, he carried this burden on his little shoulders. I felt guilty for not recognizing his grief because my own was so overwhelming.

I drew him close, and we sobbed together. I rocked him back and forth, whispering, "It's okay, it's okay."

My dad stood up, stunned, and looked at Mr. Bates as if seeking advice. Mr. Bates put his arm around Dad's shoulders and shook his head, unable to find words. Nana looked numb; she was out of tears. It was too much. All the others stared down at their feet in sadness, but no one spoke.

What could anyone possibly say to Liam? I looked at my dad and mouthed *What do I do?*

Dad came over, picked Liam up, and walked a few feet away from the crowd for a private conversation. He sat Liam on a large wooden crate and took a seat beside him. "Son, I'm sorry I didn't understand how important these adventures were to you. But you aren't going to get to heaven that way, and Mom is never coming back."

"Then how do you get there, Dad?"

"In the Bible, Jesus says, 'I am the way, the truth, and the life. No one comes to the Father except through me.' You must accept Jesus as your Lord and Savior. Then, when you die, you will be with Mom in heaven. I can pray with you right now if you'd like." Liam nodded.

The others dispersed and wandered away in sad silence to other activities. I felt a hand on my shoulder and turned to see Nana standing behind me. Her face looked worn, but she smiled and wrapped her arms around me. "You did good, sweetheart. You will make a great mom someday."

I rested my head on her shoulder. "Guess what, Nana?"

"What, baby?"

"I told Ben I loved him."

She chuckled softly.

Chapter 13:
Kidnapped

As night fell, everything was unusually quiet as everyone contemplated the events of the day. Several Egyptian workers had dashed into town to fetch a doctor. After examining Liam, Ben, and me, he determined there were no broken bones or apparent internal injuries. He recommended rest and keeping Ben's leg clean and elevated.

Ben slept most of the day while I sat by his bedside. I spent my time texting Rachel about the cave-in and Liam's breakdown. She was very supportive and sympathetic, saying she would have the whole youth group at church pray for us.

At dinner time, Nana came to the medical tent and brought us dinner. Liam came with her, barging in and interrupting our conversation. He hopped up on Ben's cot and crossed his legs.

"Are you feeling better, Ben?"

"Sure am, little buddy."

"I heard some new riddles from your dad today; he told me to come here and tell them to you."

"He probably got tired of answering your endless questions and sent you over to bother us with silly dad jokes," I said.

"Mr. Bates loves answering my questions, but those were his jokes," replied Liam. "Hmm, I wonder if he was trying to get rid of me. Nah, everybody loves hanging out with me."

Ben smiled as I rolled my eyes.

"Just, tell the jokes, will ya," I muttered.

"Okay, here goes. What kinda roads do mummies like living on? Dead ends!"

A small smile from Ben, nothing from me.

"How about this one: What kinda music do mummies listen to? Wrap music!"

Crickets.

"Really, that one was good! Okay, final one, what do you call a Pharaoh lying in the wrong pyramid? A grave mistake!"

Moans, eye rolls, Ben pleading with Liam to stop.

"Man, you guys are no fun. I'm gonna tell them to Nasir. I bet he laughs." and off Liam went.

"He's so much happier since his talk with dad," I said.

"I knew there was something different about him," replied Ben.

Ben's dad entered and took a seat in a chair. "How are you doing, kid?"

"I'm okay, Dad," he mumbled between bites of dinner. "Man, I didn't realize how hungry I was until now."

"Yeah, a near-death experience can make you kind of hungry," his dad joked.

"It also makes you tired," announced Nana, "so I expect both of you to get a good night's sleep."

"I know I will; I can barely keep my head up now," I said.

"You finish your dinner and then head out for your tent; I will sleep here tonight next to my boy," said Bill.

"Dad, I'm not two; I'll be fine without you," said Ben.

Bill hopped up on the cot beside Ben's cot, lay back, and pulled his hat over his face. "Can't hear you, son; sleeping."

Ben rolled his eyes and gave me a look of exasperation, shaking his head. Then he went back to eating his dinner without another word.

I giggled at the two of them; they were so alike.

After finishing my dinner, I kissed Ben's cheek and said good night. I went to our tent to get ready for bed. I grabbed clean clothes and headed to the shower tent to wash up. I felt so sore, with bruises all over my body. My clothes were filthy and tattered after all the debris fell on them, so they would have to be thrown away.

When I returned to the tent, I felt much better with clean hair, a clean body, and fresh clothes. The only thing I wanted now was to sleep. Inside the tent, Nana was sitting on her bed reading, while Liam chatted with Dad.

I walked past all of them, fell face down on my cot, and muttered from my pillow, "Someone, please turn out the light."

Dad smiled. "A little tired, are we?" he asked.

"Umph," was all I could say.

In just a few minutes, Dad had Liam tucked into bed and turned off the lights. I was already asleep.

Amin and his companions waited patiently for the camp to quiet down and for the lights to turn off. When they finally felt that most everyone was asleep, they gathered their belongings and took out their weapons. Amin had a gun, while the other two wielded knives.

Amin peeked through the tent flaps and signaled for the others to follow as he dashed between the tents toward the O'Connors. He felt shaky with antic-ipation at the thought of his revenge being fulfilled.

He stood by the flaps of the O'Connor tent, listening intently. All he could hear was snoring. Slowly, he moved inside and held the tent flaps back for the others to enter. He gestured with his hands to indicate where they should stand. One positioned himself over Cara's cot, while the other went to Liam's. They left Nana undisturbed.

Amin pressed his gun against Vic's head, leaned down, and whispered, "Wakey, wakey, oh Captain, my captain."

Vic jolted awake and sat up. In an instant, he felt the gun and realized that Amin had caught up with him.

"Do not make a sound! Or your children will suffer," Amin cautioned in a whisper.

Vic peered into the shadows and saw men standing beside his children's bed. His heart stopped. Inside his mind, he prayed, *Jesus, help me. Don't let him harm my kids.*

In the middle of the night, as I was in a deep sleep, I heard voices that nudged me awake. Slowly, I opened my eyes and glanced around the tent. Whose voice was that? Wait, now there were two voices; one belonged to my dad. I sat up and peered through the darkness to see a stranger holding a gun to my dad's head. Terror filled my heart. Then, someone grabbed me from behind, covering my mouth. He yanked me out of my bed. I struggled to break free as a scream involuntarily rose in my throat.

The man holding me was stronger than me, and he whispered in my ear, "Do not scream if you want your dad to live."

I stopped struggling and waited. My heart raced a hundred beats faster than normal. I glanced around the room, searching for a weapon or a means of escape. Liam and Nana were still sleeping, while a third man hovered over Liam's bed. I began to struggle again, trying to break free and help him. The man gripped tighter and angrily whispered for me to stop moving.

I heard my dad say, "Let them go. They have no connection to this. I'll go with you; just leave them alone. Please."

I struggled to speak through the hand holding my mouth shut. "Humph, no, Dad."

The other man spoke. "Oh, Captain, my captain, I cannot leave behind your family; they are my leverage for you to follow my command." Then he spoke to his men in Arabic. "*Amsikahum.*"

The man holding me dragged me toward the tent door, while the man standing over Liam and Nana snatched up Liam with one hand and pushed Nana awake with the other.

"What's going on? Who are you?" asked Nana.

192

"Hey, let go of me! Help, Dad!" yelled Liam.

"Shut up, you whelp," the man said, shaking Liam.

"It's okay, everyone. Listen to me. Don't struggle against these men; it will only make matters worse," Dad said, trying to calm us all. "We must go with Amin and his men. Don't be afraid, we won't be harmed if we do as they say."

The men moved us all toward the tent door. "Wait," said Nana, "I need my shoes."

The men stopped. "Fine," said Amin as he flipped on the light. "Find your shoes. Hurry!"

The thugs waited as we searched for our shoes and laced them up. We looked at each other for reassurance. I noticed that only the leader had a gun. I wondered how I could use this to our advantage.

Liam finished tying his shoes and slowly reached under his cot to pull out his whip. He quickly tucked it under his pajama top and stood up.

Once we had all put on our shoes, the leader motioned with his gun for us to leave the tent, instructing us to keep our hands up. They marched us over to a large truck and demanded that we get in. Nana struggled to climb in first, followed by me.

As I stood on the step leading into the second seat of the truck, I heard screaming. It was Liam, bent over, pretending to cry and wail. I wondered what on earth he was doing.

"Shut up, boy!" one of the men yelled. Suddenly,

Liam jumped up and slammed into the man's face with his head, breaking his nose and causing him to fall to the ground, screaming in pain. Then, he whipped around to face Amin, drew his whip, and snapped it around Amin's gun, snatching it out of his hand and sending it flying behind the truck. It happened so quickly that Amin was unable to respond.

At the same time, I leaped from the truck and landed on another man's back, knocking him flat, while Dad seized Amin, causing them both to tumble to the ground. In seconds, they were punching and kicking, brawling like wild animals in a desperate fight for survival.

Liam struck the man with a broken nose, whipping him relentlessly. The man attempted to block the blows and grab the end of the whip, but Liam was too swift. The man rose to his feet and fled while Liam pursued him, fearless and shouting a war cry.

I was thrown off the back of the man I'd grabbed as he turned to pin me down. I fought like a wildcat, scratching, kicking, and screaming bloody murder. The next thing I knew, he was out cold, falling onto his side next to the truck. I looked up, and Nana was holding a tire iron.

"Good job, Nana!" I yelled before hopping up to see what else was happening.

Dad was still whaling away at Amin, the man with the broken nose was running for the gate, and a dozen people who had heard our commotion were racing toward us, including several armed guards.

Within moments, the guards were pointing their weapons at Amin and his accomplices, barking orders at them in Arabic. Amin and the man with the broken nose dropped to their knees with their arms in the air, while the man Nana had knocked down remained unconscious.

Dad stepped back as the guards took control. He rushed over to us, and the four of us grouped together in a hug, all asking at once if everyone was okay.

Ben, Bill, and several others arrived, and after reassuring them that we were okay, Dad began to recount the story of Amin and his plan for revenge.

Once the Egyptian authorities took the men away, everything returned to normal. After visiting the medical tent for some minor first aid, we all returned to our tents.

As I lay in bed, I asked Dad, "Dad, why didn't you tell us about these guys?"

"Sweetheart, I didn't want you all to worry. I thought Amin was locked up in jail until I made that call to the ship. Besides, it's my job to protect you, and that's what I was trying to do."

"I wanna protect us too!" declared Liam.

"Me too!" said Nana.

"Me too," I said.

Dad sighed.

"Okay, okay. If there's another threat, I'll let you know. That way, Liam can grab his whip, Nana can get her tire iron, and Cara, well, she'll sharpen her nails. Did you see the scratches she put on that guy?"

We all laughed.

Chapter 14:
Final Chapter or Just Beginning?

Ben and I walked around the camp. It was essential for him to exercise his injured leg, so I ensured he walked every day.

"These last few days have been so quiet," I said to Ben, "Liam hasn't tried to sneak off on any adventures at all. Every night, we've sat together as a family and talked about Mom. We've been sharing stories about her, laughing and crying together. It's been very healing. My dad said we would continue to do this every year and never forget her."

"I'm so happy for you, Cara. This must be an answer to some of your prayers."

"I never thought about it, but yes. Yes, it is an answer to my prayers. However, another prayer still needs to be answered."

"Oh yeah, what's that?"

"I'm praying for your complete recovery, which won't happen if you don't continue your physical therapy every day, mister!"

"Man, you are so bossy!"

Dad approached. "Cara, can I interrupt? I need to speak with you in private for a few minutes."

"Sure. Ben, I'll be right back. Keep walking!"

Dad and I walked to the family tent, where Nana and Liam waited patiently. "So what's up, Dad?" Liam asked.

"I got a call from the Navy on the satellite phone." My heart began to race. This was it. Dad was going back to the ship early. Perhaps there was an emergency or an act of war. I was afraid to know, but I had to know. Nana and Liam must have been thinking the worst, too, because they inhaled sharply and held their breath.

Dad saw the fear on our faces and smiled. "Don't worry. It's good news. Several months ago, I applied to be transferred back to Yorktown. But I was denied. When I called the ship to report all that had happened this week, I spoke to my superior, and he said he would approve my transfer after all. He said our family has been through enough. I'm coming home!"

No one moved. There was complete silence for thirty seconds. "Wait, you mean you don't have to return to your ship?" I asked tentatively.

"Well, I need to go back until the end of the month to pack up my gear and meet the new captain, but after that, I'll be home to stay."

Another thirty seconds of silence, and then the explosion.

"Hallelujah!" yelled Nana.

I just screamed.

Liam jumped up and down, yelling, "Yes, yes, yes!"

We made such a racket that people came from all directions to see what was happening. They rushed into the tent to find us laughing, jumping, hugging, yelling, and celebrating. We reassured them that we were okay and shared the good news, after which they joined us in our celebration. I left the group and ran to tell Ben.

"Ben! Dad has been reassigned to Yorktown, Virginia. He's coming home!" I threw my arms around him and planted a big kiss on his lips. He responded appropriately.

Bill walked in. "Um, excuse me, you two." Ben and I broke away from each other. "I just heard the great news, Cara. But before you go, Ben tells me you have a journal where you've recorded the past two weeks."

"Yes, sir. I love writing in my journal. I want to write a book someday about Liam's wild adventures."

"Why wait for someday? I started my career

by writing a book about my travel adventures. My mentor at the time was a famous archaeologist who helped me develop, edit, and publish my book. I would love to see you succeed in your career by paying it forward."

"You mean you want to be my mentor and help me write a book!"

"Yep!"

I had to sit down. I was blown away. "Wow, that would be amazing, Mr. Bates. I'd love to!"

"Great, let me see your journal."

"Um, no, those are my private thoughts, and you cannot read them."

"Oh, I won't tell anyone. I just want to see what we have to work with," he said. "Come on, let's go to your tent and fetch the journal."

"Yeah, Cara, show my dad your journal. I want to see it too," Ben grinned. I was horrified at the thought of Ben reading my journal.

Liam rushed in and jumped between us, saying, "Hey! If my sister doesn't want you to touch her journal, you'd better leave it alone!" He threatened Bill with his whip raised. "Back off, Bates!"

I covered my smile with my hand and tried to sound angry. "Yeah, back off, Bates!"

Bill laughed. "Okay, okay, little guy, don't snap that thing at me; I was just teasing your sister."

So, my little brother was living up to his name: strong-willed warrior.

We all laughed. "So, Cara, I was serious about the mentorship. When would you like to start?"

And so, my next adventure began...

Dear Journal,

It's been four years since the day we appeared on The Today Show. *I remember being extremely nervous; I sweated so much that I didn't dare raise my arms for fear of large wet circles under them.*

Liam, Ben, and Bill seemed very comfortable and chatted nonstop. Fortunately, the host rarely asked me any questions. However, when she did, she asked how I was feeling. All I could think of was thanking God for granting me the ability to write, and then I smiled.

When it was over, I was relieved that I hadn't thrown up. I thought I could relax now because there would be no more cameras and lights in my face, no more news crews asking me questions and trailing behind me with microphones. I was mistaken.

After that interview, my life was never the same. Ben lives in Gloucester now, and we are dating. We spent a lot of time on trips with his dad. I've appeared on the Exploring the Ancients *show many times and have continued to collaborate on additional books with Bill. Since he is a big celebrity, I have become a sort of shadow celebrity, along with Ben.*

We can't go anywhere without cameras in our faces. People want selfies with us and even ask for my autograph. All these experiences make me uncomfortable. But I use these opportunities to encourage others to share their gifts. I can share Jesus with more people and even pray with those who seem like they need a friend.

Ben graduated two years ago and has a fantastic job at the marine biology lab here in Gloucester. Bill includes him in any adventure he has planned, whether it's marine-related or involves underwater exploration.

Liam is just starting at Gloucester High School, channeling his boundless curiosity and energy into sports and the robotics club. He no longer feels the need to embark on solo misadventures; instead, he frequently joins Bill's crew for adventures. Sometimes, he even invites his buddy Danny to tag along.

Dad and Nana enjoy staying at home and are actively involved in our local church activities. Dad's commute to work is only about ten minutes now, which is great. We spend a lot of time together, and the shadow of grief has lifted from our family. Sometimes, I think my mom and Jesus planned this wild adventure to Egypt just to heal our sorrow.

Ben began attending church with me. He committed his life to Jesus at the altar, and I am pleased to say we are now equally yoked. Ben and I are engaged and will marry this fall after I graduate from college.

We haven't chosen a date yet for the wedding. It seems that Bill has a great adventure he's planning, and he wants us to be there with him. I assume he intends this to be another book, and he wants me to take notes while there. However, he hasn't worked out the dates yet, so until he does, we can't solidify our wedding plans.

Bill won't even tell us where he's planning to go. I hope his plans don't turn into a misadventure. I really don't want to trudge through muddy jungles, sweat out in the desert, chase weird (sometimes imaginary) creatures, or get caught in a cave-in right before my wedding day. But whatever his plans, I want to go. The adventure bug is in my soul, thanks to Liam.

Anyway, my friend Rachel beat me to the altar and is expecting her first baby. I'm throwing her baby shower this week. I can't wait to see the new baby. Rachel will be my maid of honor, while Liam will be Ben's best man.

I'm excited about the new baby, I can't wait

for the wedding, and I'm even thrilled to be invited on another adventure traveling with Bill Bates and crew. I have never been happier.

Best of all, dear Journal, Ben and I now create our bucket list together.

Other great reads from Dee Ouellette...

Zoo At School

What would happen if a chimpanzee appeared in your high school gym? Or a lion in the cafeteria? Or maybe a rhino in the janitor's closet?

Zoo at School is an adventure from the first page to the last. Anna and her friends volunteer at a small animal sanctuary called Chic-a-Ta Zoo. The teens get to know the exotic animals and their unique personalities, including Sampson the Lion, Bertha the Elephant, and Harry the Chimp. However, not everyone loves the zoo. A deliberate act of sabotage leaves the cages open and the animals loose, causing them to end up at the local high school.

The town declares the animals dangerous and decides they must be euthanized. But the teens devise a plan to save them. They must herd them north to Freedom Ranch, a large animal sanctuary where they can live out their lives in peace.

However, the town council president is determined to seek revenge and hires a posse to pursue and kill the animals. Will the animals reach safety, or will they be shot along the way?

Ty & Jake Adventures: The Lost Gold Mine

Tyler is forced into a family vacation he doesn't want to take but soon discovers a hundred-year-old mystery remains unsolved.

He enlists his younger brother Jake and eventually his entire family to search for clues.

He doesn't realize that someone is lurking in the background, watching and waiting to seize the treasure if it's found—someone dangerous with a score to settle.

In this first tale of the Ty & Jake Adventure Series, you will find it all—drama, adventure, danger, villains, and even skeletons!

Available at Amazon, Barnes and Noble, or on the author's website: www.deeouellette.com